T0016229

PRAISE FOR *NINTH BU*

". . . [I]n this limpid translation by Jeremy Tiang, there is an obser-vational richness to the stories that humanises them and defeats the regime's attempt to depersonalise lived experience. A fine book that stands with other quality works about the Cultural Revolution by writers such as Yan Lianke and Zhang Xianliang.

—*The Irish Times*

"*Ninth Building* is a truly unique piece of literature that gives us a series of glimpses into the mind and experiences of a young man before he grew into one of China's most celebrated aritsts."

—Books & Bao

NINTH BUILDING
Zou Jingzhi

Translated by Jeremy Tiang

OPEN LETTER
LITERARY TRANSLATIONS FROM THE UNIVERSITY OF ROCHESTER

Originally published in Chinese as 九栋 by 法律出版社
Copyright © Zou Jingzhi 2010
Translation copyright © Jeremy Tiang 2022, 2023

This translation first published by Honford Star, 2022
honfordstar.com

First Open Letter edition, 2023
All rights reserved

Library of Congress Cataloging-in-Publication Data: Available.
ISBN (pb): 978-1-948830-75-1 | ISBN (eBook): 978-1-948830-88-1

Printed on acid-free paper in the United States of America.

Cover design by Eric Wilder

Open Letter is the University of Rochester's nonprofit, literary translation press:
Dewey Hall 1-219, Box 278968, Rochester, NY 14627

www.openletterbooks.org

CONTENTS

NINTH BUILDING

INTRODUCTION

Dreaming, waking, sunrise, time to get up. The person in the dream was a bit different to the person I am now, but I think it was me. I try to go back but can't.

From childhood till now, I've spoken many bold words. Publicly or in private, I've proclaimed the kind of person I wanted to be, though it never happened in the end. I feel like someone has somehow taken my place, leaving me to become the person I am now.

When I'm around too many people, I lose myself. In an unfamiliar city, among crowds of strangers, I keep having to stand still—not to ask directions, but to find myself. Even when I've done that, I'm still lonely, so I head back to my hotel and listen to the sound of rain.

Apart from my mortal body, I carry around a compilation of shadows, leaving one behind everywhere I go. The other day, I went to admire some flowers, when a shadow abruptly stepped out from behind a magnolia tree of a decade ago. It was me. We looked at each other, speechless. The trees hadn't changed, the flowers hadn't changed, the springtime hadn't changed, but when I looked at myself, I saw a stranger.

I went to a gathering where I only knew a few people. Picked a corner to sit alone. Shortly afterwards, someone in the same plight joined me for a chat. We grew animated. Meanwhile, the real me also sat in that corner, watching this babbling self and loathing him.

Other people are always borrowing me. My wife says, "It's sunny today, come to the mall with me—I want to buy socks." Yes, dear. Then I have to leave myself at home for three hours, to await my return.

While waiting for my daughter to be born, I laid siege to the delivery room. Suddenly, there was a thunderous howl. Definitely my child. I looked through the glass at the infant, who stared back at me. A moment of recognition.

I look at old photos of myself when I was simple and pure as the sky above me. After a while, both of us begin to weep, and it's hard to say which era of our lives was better. All time will vanish. No more looking at pictures, that other me doesn't want his heartstrings tugged at either.

Reading Zhang Ruoxu's poem "Springtime River Moonlit Night," "Who first saw the moon from this riverbank? When did the river moon first shine upon a person?" The man on the riverbank turns to glance at me, and the strangeness in that gaze is chilling.

I walk alone through snowy plains. I could laugh or sob or sing or curse or fall silent or sprint or roll across the ground. In an instant, many selves appear, like a carnival crowd. At the same time, people appear in the distance and engulf me. And there I am gaping blankly, standing between white snow and blue sky, snot streaming from my nose.

My hand grips a pen and the pen writes words. When I'm done, another me springs from my heart to read it over and say it's all lies. Why am I lying to myself? Good question. Really good question.

I buy books and don't read them, or I do but actually I'm listening to people chat outside my window, to wind and trees and ghosts and rain. *Whap!* The book smacks my head as I doze off.

A beautiful woman passes by. I look, I don't look, I'm in a state of looking and not looking. As for her, she both displays and doesn't display contempt for me.

Late at night, I stare mindlessly at a lone star. After some time, I feel that I've always been ancient, or perhaps that was a past life. The wind tugs at my sleeves. Someone is very close to me. I shut my eyes, so I don't have to see who it is.

A fever. I float over the edge of a cliff and startle awake. Float some more. Jerk awake again. Why always these terrifying scenarios? To put myself in a cold sweat. It's a way of helping myself. If I weren't able to do that, I'd drift till I hit bottom, finally, the most terrifying word that goes unsaid.

PART ONE:
NINTH BUILDING

PROLOGUE

Ninth Building was the building I lived in as a child. It's been demolished now, and on the same plot they built a bigger, taller Ninth Building. My words only concern the previous incarnation.

Before the block disappeared, I went back to take some pictures of it. A place I spent my early years. With its vanishing, there'd be no traces left of my childhood.

In the second half of 1996, after the demolition, I began writing these words, producing a first draft of over a hundred thousand characters. I edited four of these stories into shape, and they were published in 1997, along with a few other pieces in journals. In the summer of 1999, I started editing a dozen more in fits and starts, which still left half the manuscript untouched. I originally wrote this book with the idea that by putting them on paper, these past events would release their hold on me. Instead, it felt as if I'd cemented their grip. Having written them out simply made their shadowing more visible.

That's why I edited this manuscript below, then left it alone. To me, publishing these words is essentially me sharing my treasured childhood with others. But childhood cannot be shared. Her secret parts must remain eternally secret. Even if you try to recall it with your whole heart and mind, you'd find it hard to go back in.

EIGHT DAYS

Freezing today—it feels extra cold, because the weather's just turned. At least it's warm at home, with the heating finally on. In the morning, we sat by the courtyard wall, the south-facing corner with the piles of loose soil and torn paper, the only patch untouched by the wind.

By "we" I mean myself, Zheng Chao, Zheng Xin, and Yuanqiang. Yuanqiang said the others had formed a unit and got Red Guard armbands printed with the official insignia. Now they were occupying an entire block at the school. At night they shoved the desks together and slept on them. They'd written slogans across the white classroom walls and even the toilets. While correcting Teacher Hou's thinking, they struck up a chant that Tian Shuhua devised: "Ho ho, Monkey Hou, holds a ball in her hole. Smile, monkey, drop the ball."

Teacher Hou teaches Chinese. I saw her recently, standing by the second-story staircase. No one was paying any attention to her. As I walked past, she was singing a song about a sad maiden, something to do with resisting the Japanese.

I had a strange feeling that when she was done singing, she'd plummet to the ground. I waited, but she didn't jump. Her son sat at the other end of the corridor, pretending to play but really watching

5

her. She once praised me for having talent. (I should delete that last sentence—too bourgeois!)

After talking about it all morning, we decided to form a unit of our own. Yuanqiang said there was a place to print armbands near Caishikou, past a place called Dazhi Bridge. There were many gangsters in that neighborhood; last time the guys were there, they got mugged and lost three yuan. Zheng Xin said he'd bring a carving tool with him. It wasn't a knife, but it was still sharp enough to slice open a face. I felt heartened by his words.

We prepared to set off the next day, as soon as the grown-ups left for work. We pooled our money and came up with five yuan, one of them mine.

November 17

Today, we took the number one bus to Xidan. I was the only one who had a ticket, the other three slipped on without one. I did too, but spent the whole journey fretting and in the end bought one just before getting off. What an idiot!

From Xidan we headed south, growing anxious as we neared Dazhi Bridge. I put my hand in my trouser pocket, which held a weight from a set of scales—hopefully this would be hefty enough to dent a gangster's head. It sat cold and heavy in my pocket. I couldn't warm it. Zheng Xin whistled as he strolled, a hand inside his jacket. The carving tool he held was our heartbeat.

The event we feared never happened. The wind was so strong we had to jog along.

Past Dazhi Bridge, we walked into a rope shop to ask directions to the fabric-printing place. The old man told us where, some hutong or other.

This was the first time I smelled dye. We detected it some distance away. Later, I learned this was the odor of yellow. Each color had its own scent. Yellow's reminded me of illness. A young lady served us. She reminded me of Liu Naiping's older sister from Door Three, who'd worn a red swimsuit the one time I went swimming with her. I believed then that only female college students should be called young ladies, and even then, only ones like Zoya. Liu Hulan didn't resemble one, nor did Zhu Yingtai, nor did my own sister.

She wore a face mask, only revealing her eyes, but I could tell when she was smiling. All four of us were a little tense, a little awkward.

We ordered twenty-one armbands, four inches wide with gold lettering, twenty cents each. That was as many as we could afford—I think she realized that.

As she wrote out our receipt, the kettle on the stove behind her began bubbling, *zrr, zrr.* The room was draped with pennants displaying various words and pictures, the bright red fabric bearing down on us from all four walls.

I thought of the illustration of d'Artagnan kneeling to kiss the queen in *The Three Musketeers.* The queen's feet were invisible beneath her long dress, her hand on her puffed-out skirt, d'Artagnan's lips just touching her fingertips. I always felt this was something I'd do when I was grown up. (Strike this paragraph—too bourgeois.)

She smiled and asked if we'd like to have a look at the workshop. We said yes.

The room she led us into had liquid sloshing across the floor. The workers glanced at us. I didn't understand what was going on. The printed cloths were still sodden red, and on each of them were the words "Red Guards," over and over, covered with a layer of rice chaff. She explained that this protected the color. The chaff was removed when the cloth had dried, leaving an even brighter yellow.

It was noon and we had nothing to eat, so she shared her packed lunch with us. She'd brought it from home and left it on the stove to keep warm. It contained just rice, cabbage and tofu. Not much of a meal.

By the time we left, she still hadn't taken off her face mask. She was very neat. We hadn't had a chance to see what she looked like.

Nothing went wrong on the bus home. We slipped aboard through the doors on either side, saving the fare—we'd spend that on our return trip to pick up the armbands.

Before we said goodbye, Yuanqiang asked me if I could guess the young lady's family background. I had no idea. He said, Probably capitalist. I asked why. He said, Didn't you see how beautiful she was, also she was wearing a face mask—afraid of the stench of the dye. That made sense.

November 19

More and more people are wearing Red Guard armbands in the street, and ours aren't ready yet. During the day we're at Zheng Chao's place. We don't want to go out—too conspicuous without armbands. Something might have happened to Zheng Chao and Zheng Xin's father. I saw him in the boiler room carrying heavy radiators, but the two of them didn't say a word about him.

November 20

Zheng Chao and Zheng Xin's dad is in real trouble.

We stayed home this morning, desperate for our armbands to be ready so we could rise up and maybe even denounce our parents. My older brother stuck a big poster on the wall: "Revolution is not wrong, rising up is correct." The atmosphere at home is a bit tense.

November 21

Two more days . . .

November 23

On the bus this morning, we all got caught by the ticket inspector. She wanted to take us to Central Station. We were all shaking, then so many people got on at Wangfujing that we managed to slip away. Too scared to try another bus, we walked all the way to Caishikou.

We picked up our twenty-one armbands.

The young lady looked different from six days ago. She had a scarf over her head as she mopped the workshop floor. (Later we realized someone must have shaved her head.) A piece of white cloth sewn across her chest proclaimed "Bourgeois traitor Liu Liyuan." She still wore her face mask, and all the time she served us, kept her head lowered. In six days she'd been transformed into an ancient crone.

Like before, the stove held a kettle, along with her lunchbox.

A man walked in to make tea. He ordered her to remove her mask. She was motionless for a moment before plucking it off.

She looked as I'd imagined, very pale, like a picture never seen before.

As we walked away, she was already picking up her broom again. She said "goodbye" softly when we left. The mask dangled in front of her chest, not hiding the white cloth. I read the words again swiftly—Yuanqiang had been right, she was a capitalist.

A person inscribed with words became those words, and nothing more than those words. As we walked down the street, I noticed more and more people had been labeled. Even some of the Red Guards were burdened with this white cloth and black lettering. Everyone was just a row of characters.

We put on our armbands as soon as we emerged from the hutong. Our arms grew glorious, weighty. Only swinging them vigorously made them feel natural.

Swaggering, we strutted into a small eating house and ordered four portions of roast meat. We splayed the food open, pouring soy sauce and vinegar in great streams that splashed across the table. The waiter saw the mess we were creating but didn't dare say a word. Our arms moved stiffly, as if we'd just been vaccinated.

GARBAGE CART

Yes, come and see, this is the downfall of the landlord class. She was a landlady, my stepmother, she's dead now, killed herself, slit her throat with scissors, slowly sliced it open, so blood splashed on the wall, you can see how it squirted all over, even in death she had to do the wrong thing, why would she want to die in this house, why did she have to bleed so much, enough to drown a family, enough to drown them dead? (Here, he burst into tears.)

When we're dead we get cremated, but where should she go now, who'd be willing to drag this she-landlord, her entire body soaked in blood, all the way to the mortuary? No one, no comrade of the Revolution would do such a thing, I understand, I'm not willing either, but even Hell can only be reached through the crematorium chimney, am I right? Revolutionary comrades, help me open the gates of Hades, let cow demons and snake spirits swarm in, unleash the torments of fire and whipping and knives and water, no hope of liberation for all eternity.

Come! Little generals of the Revolution, go find a rickshaw, never mind if it has no engine, I'll pull it, I'll move it with these hands dripping with the fresh blood of landlords. I want to send her to hell, after all we can't let the dark spirit of the landlord class linger here, can we? Rise up, overthrow landlords! She can't hear me, but her blood is still flowing. Comrades, even a handcart would do, even the one from the morning trash collection. Please, I beg you, help me find one, I'll pull it twenty li if it gets her to the crematorium. No! First I'll wrap her in white cloth so her filthy blood doesn't soil our socialist roads.

Do something, little generals of the Revolution, let this landlord scum be blown away as ashes and smoke! Observe her wounds, not just one cut but many, how could she have brought herself to do it, slit her neck with her own hands, not like slaughtering chickens, not an accident, this was deliberate, the determination of the landlord class, she'd made up her mind to die. None of us realized last night as she drank her bowl of rice porridge, the slushy sound of congee slipping through the toothless crack—where'd she get the strength to cut herself to death?

Where's the cart? Why haven't the gates to hell opened yet? I can't wait anymore, I can't let the death of one demon affect the progress of the Revolution. Faster, little generals, faster!

She cut herself to death.

You there, please take care, don't let Chen Zhe and Chen Yu barge in here. They were brought up by their granny, I don't want them to see this, our lives completely changed, what are we going to do about this bloodstained wall, cover it, plaster it, but it'll still be there, just that we can't see it, it's turning darker, reddish brown, not like blood any more, but still there, you see how forcefully the blood gushed out, look at this, look here, how it splashed, she was already more than sixty years old, but her blood still had such strength in it, yes it did!

Overthrow the landlord class! If the landlords won't surrender, let them be exterminated! Good, well shouted.

No! You don't need to take any action against me, I'm her adopted son, an orphan, I'm a child with no status, the blood that flows in my veins might come from a warrior of the Autumn Harvest Uprising, last year someone tried to verify my ancestry, they did! So I might be a martyr's orphan, really I have more reason than any of you to desire

Revolution, I've always yearned for Revolution, and now it's finally here, but I'll admit I wasn't sufficiently prepared, I didn't think it would be like this.

Why hasn't a cart been found yet? In the name of the Revolution, I urge you to hurry! As a descendant of an old Revolutionary, I ask—I even order you—what? If you need the key, go find the old guy who collects the rubbish, he's at Yangfangdian number seventeen, go quickly, cycle there!

Come along, little generals, we can't just stand here gaping, we ought to swiftly eliminate the traces of the landlord class, we won't leave a shred behind, can someone go fetch some sawdust, yes, we'll cover the blood first, and if we dare we'll scrape each bloodstain off the wall, we'll put all this behind us as quickly as possible, we won't let the enemy affect the Revolution, come on, little generals, let's see whose Revolutionary spirit is the strongest.

Let's call out, "Overthrow . . ."

That's right, we'll rip the plaster off the wall, never mind if the concrete shows through, don't worry, this is the enemy's blood, we should treat it with hatred, come, let's sing the Chairman's quotations, my Revolutionary spirit isn't as strong as yours, I haven't memorized enough of them, but starting tomorrow, I'll throw myself wholeheartedly into the Revolution, yes. First I'll learn the words, then I'll broadcast them in the streets.

Hey! Don't touch her, she's already dead, let her be, let her rest where she is, don't touch, let's tidy up, get rid of the bloodstains. That's better, more like a regular death, not a gruesome suicide. Why did she have to do this? Less mess if she'd hanged herself. Why the hell scissors? What was she trying to show? Some sort of womanly tenderness, or callousness?

Did she have to die? She was just a landlord's mistress, little revolutionary generals, just a mistress, she spent half her life being oppressed too, wearing tattered clothes and eating bad food, she was brought here by boat from Yuanjiang City and sold to the landlord, when he died she continued collecting rents in his name, she did, but she also suffered humiliation from her clan, and after Liberation, this all had to be surrendered, leaving her with nothing. When I was at university, she supported me by unraveling and winding yarn, hands covered in scars and feet always swollen, her wounds were my sustenance all through college, and now I'm a cadre, a Beijing cadre, from a starving orphan to a cadre in Beijing, and she was by my side every single day, now she's dead, cut herself to death with scissors, like a bolt of lightning her death strikes my body, I feel a little sad now, like I should cry, howl loudly, but I won't get in the way of your slogans, please shout away, she can't hear anything now, and to think last night she was drinking her congee with a sound like innumerable words being choked away, now I think she must have swallowed everything she wanted to say.

The cart is here, good the garbage cart, garbage cart, garb—no, I'm fine, but I've changed my mind, I, I'm going to request a van, a clean van with Liberation license plates, I can't let her travel all that way lying in a garbage cart, you can say what you like, I'm not afraid, but this won't do, I can't let her go like this, I have the right, I might be the orphan of a martyr, no, no, I won't put her in this cart.

Chen Zhe, Chen Yu, come in, come in, I've covered up her wounds, come see your granny. One last look.

CAPTURING THE SPOON

While on patrol around midnight on the eighteenth of October, we noticed a light in Wang Hao's home. There were five of us: Jinjing, White Monkey, Little Jianzi, Zhang Liang and me. We wanted to see what they were up to so late at night. The whole building was in darkness except for that one ground-floor apartment.

The blinds only covered half the window. It wasn't hard to see inside.

Wang Hao's dad was naked, thrashing around on top of Wang Hao's mom. It took us a moment to realize she was naked too. We could see everything so clearly, it felt fake. They squirmed against each other, chatting about putting money aside to buy a bicycle. All five of us witnessed this, and when we were sure what was going on, we retreated.

Two grown-ups from our compound's "Attack With Words, Defend With Force" Unit were working the night shift. When we knocked on the door, they were both there sporting their red armbands. One was in the middle of a story about a work trip. He was smoking and kept interrupting himself to draw on his cigarette, not in any hurry. He saw us come in but didn't stop his anecdote, something about being on a train and buying a box lunch, and the meat that came in it being as thin as paper. When he said "paper," he pinched two fingers together. We didn't know what to say to this, so we sat and stared at each other, uncertain how to bring the matter up.

Finally, Jinjing interrupted. "Wang Hao's home still has a light on." He looked down and fiddled with his pockets, adding, "Their lamp is on."

"Not asleep?" said the smoking man.

"Not asleep," said two or three of us at the same time.

"Do you know what they're up to?" The other man had been reading a mimeographed news sheet, but now looked up at us.

"His dad, his mom, they're . . . they're naked."

"They're doing . . . bad things."

We were stammering so much, the business of putting money aside to buy a bicycle didn't even come up. We waited. The two grown-ups barely moved. One of them clearly wanted to finish his story about the boxed lunch, and the other continued to flip the newssheet. They didn't seem to think what we'd seen was important.

Nothing came of our waiting. We'd imagined they would jump up immediately to stop whatever incorrect action was taking place. This was at the height of the Revolution, and the train we were on had switched to another track. What we'd seen didn't fit the scenery on this route; red armbands and nakedness didn't go together. The five of us had three flashlights between us, and for more than half a month now we'd stayed awake night after night, fully alert, wishing something would actually happen. Now something had, but the adults didn't seem to feel about it the same way we did.

It was like the day before, when we caught a night-shift worker from Beijing Steelworks. When White Monkey spotted him, he had an empty aluminum lunchbox going *gwodong gwodong*, and he walked down the street ringing out *gwodong gwodong*. We were both excited and afraid when we stopped him, because he didn't show any panic, which only made him seem like one of those calm villains. He didn't have the oily, mucky, large hands a worker ought to have— he was sturdy and small. The *gwodong* racket was from a stainless steel spoon in his lunchbox. When we first heard it, I had actually thought it might be a spoon, but then quashed the thought, because no matter how you told the story, it sounded ludicrous to capture a stainless steel spoon in the middle of the night.

The "Attack With Words, Defend With Force" Unit let that guy go when dawn arrived. They even shook hands, and before the man walked away, he asked, "Is there anywhere around here to buy dough fritters?" White Monkey told him, "At the entrance of the Railway Hospital." He left, pulling the spoon from his lunchbox and placing it in his shirt pocket, so there was no further noise as he walked, only silence.

Quiet nights provided the atmosphere we needed, the atmosphere of Revolution, so we had to do something about Wang Hao's family.

The two red armband men finally muttered something about continuing our patrol, without mentioning Wang Hao's mom and dad. As we walked out, we felt as if the grown-ups had some kind of secret they were keeping from us, which made the rest of that night's sentry duty somewhat depressing.

Anyway their lamp was out by the time we reemerged, leaving the entire block in darkness.

We walked around the courtyard with our flashlights, and Jinjing said, "I saw his mom squeezing her legs together. That wasn't how I imagined it. Dammit, I know about this sort of thing, it's just not the right time for it. Think about it, two days ago Hong Jiong's dad jumped from the roof of their building, and Wang Hao's mom saw the body, I remember calling out 'Auntie' as I walked past her. Her face was white as a pagoda flower and her whole body was trembling, like she was completely shocked. Damn difficult to imagine getting from that moment to tonight so quickly. And the bicycle—it was her, wasn't it, who said they should put money away for a bicycle? What do they want with a bicycle?"

"It was her talking about the bicycle and saving money. Wang Hao's dad didn't say anything." As I spoke, I flicked my flashlight on and off. When it was lit, the world suddenly appeared, and when it went out, I couldn't see anything, didn't even know where Jinjing was standing. Facing the black night, I asked, "If you know about these things, could you tell us?"

No answer. I had plenty more questions. Jinjing didn't say anything, and nor did the rest of the group. I felt that of the five of us, some understood while others were like me, totally ignorant.

From behind, I shone my light at their backs. Everyone seemed weighed down. This night, we'd moved away from the Revolution.

The next afternoon, as I sat on the steps, I saw Wang Hao's dad coming home. He carried an ordinary black bag and wore glasses, a serious man with an air of accomplishment and responsibility. Thinking of the previous night, the wobble of his naked swaying buttocks, so different to his stern face, I felt the happiness of having seen through a secret, a joy that flickered through my heart. I ran after his gray-blue jacket that was about to disappear through the doorway.

"Bicycle!" I shouted after him. I hadn't planned to holler at him like that. How I longed for him to turn his head. But, no. He vanished, and I heard his front door open and shut.

Bicycle. From then on, that's what we called him.

SPECIMENS

My specimen collection, wedged inside a magazine, got sold to the rag-and-bone man. It consisted of three or four morning glory blossoms, five or six dragonflies, as well as three different breeds of cockroach and the feet of a dead hen. Fang Yong cut off those feet with scissors and dried them in the sun, before presenting them to me. All these things were preserved inside a journal of the technical economy, which also contained pictures of apartment blocks just like the one I lived in, Ninth Building.

I sold them in front of Ninth Building, Door Three.

At the moment of the transaction, I'd expected the man to flip through the magazine and was looking forward to his rage and shock as flowers and insects tumbled out. Perhaps he would stamp on them? But no. He only looked at the cover and tossed it onto his scales along with the rest. Three jin, including the weight of those specimens.

Maybe those old magazines ended up in a junkyard somewhere, and in the night stray cats would drag them out, moonlight gleaming in their eyes as they flicked the pages with their tongues, and when they found them, gnawing those dried chicken feet beneath the stars, *crunch crunch crunch.* My specimens would turn into food, like the dry-pickled vegetables I enjoyed.

*

A squished mosquito is a drop of blood. Once, I used a rolled-up newspaper to kill a mosquito, flattening it against the wall. When it had dried out the next day, there was nothing left but a couple of lines like an ink smear. I never collected mosquito specimens. If I had, sticking them in rows on a sheet of white paper, they'd have looked from a distance like a poem. Sounded like it too: wénzi (mosquito) and wénzì (words).

Qiao Xiaobing asked me to accompany him to the savings center on Lishi Road to withdraw some money. I said I would, but he'd have to let me look at his pet lizards.

From beneath his bed, he pulled out a cardboard box containing a thick hardcover book that had been hollowed out. Lined up neatly in the space were two medicine bottles of the type usually found in clinics, each of which held a lizard.

He brandished these, and I could clearly see the four-legged snakes' white bellies pressing against the glass as they breathed shallowly. When they looked at me, their eyes were absolutely unwavering.

"Of course they're alive. They were tiny when I caught them, and now they've grown too big to crawl out of the bottles. I feed them flies every day, live houseflies. I pluck their wings off and stuff them in, and they get swallowed up quick as lightning. Four-legged snakes have no facial expressions, only when they eat something their cheeks puff up a bit. Have you seen an insect with only one wing? It tries to fly with just that side of its body, so it goes in circles, but can't take off. It's fun to watch. The faster it tries to move, the more it's stuck."

I asked if the lizards ever took a shit. "Sure, I just pour the crap out."

He put the bottles away and said, "We should go, it's almost noon."

Before we left, he shouted behind him, "Sis, I'm going out, I'll be back around noon. Have lunch without me."

We walked about forty minutes to get there. His right hand was stuffed into his pocket, where I knew he had a passbook with five hundred yuan in savings. Before his mom and dad were caught, they sewed that passbook into his trousers. His dad was Qiao Binghao, his mom was Cui Hong. They were both spies and had been detained two months ago.

He said the day they were taken, he'd been waiting downstairs to swap his bronze hook for Fang Yong's yellow marble. He saw a bunch of grown-ups painting a slogan on the garage wall. They pasted white paper over the surface, then wrote the words one after another. First, "Overthrow Central Committee scum." He thought this was a strange thing to say, then he saw the character "Qiao," but didn't imagine it had anything to do with him. When they wrote "Bing" after it, he started to think it might be his dad, but didn't expect them to write "Cui" next. So his mom was marked too. Then a big red cross after the black words. He said he didn't have any thoughts at the time, only he forgot all about the swap with the marble.

When he headed home, he saw his sister watching him from the window.

"Her face was blank as a mirror." As he spoke, his right hand guarded his pocket.

"From that time, she never came downstairs again. I've always been close to my sister. When she was younger, she used to talk nonsense and say we'd get married when we were grown up. Silly. I've always known—this is incorrect thinking, you know that too— but I've always known she was my little sister, more important than myself. You know what I mean?" The first place we went was wrong. The clerk said this is Bank Branch Number One, you want Number Two. I started to regret agreeing to walk this far with him. His lizards weren't as great as other people seemed to think.

I asked, "Where are your mom and dad now?"

He said, "I don't know, they might be dead. Spies in the movies always die in the end."

"Were they really spies?"

"Maybe. I used to hear them talking about it all the time, on and on. You know they've both been to the Soviet Union, even our radio at home is Russian, and so's the record player and my sister's violin. When the Russian expert visited, he came to our house. I have a picture of me being hugged by a man in a Western suit. He's tall and fat, and I remember he reeked of alcohol. I smell it whenever I look at that photo. He gave me a Russian name, Vasily, but it didn't stick. While he was hugging me, he must have been thinking of another little boy called Vasily."

We filled in two withdrawal forms before getting it right. The grown-up at the window asked if he was sure he wanted to clear out the account, and he said yes. She said it was so much money, why hadn't an adult come to collect it? He said they just hadn't. She handed over five hundred yuan plus interest and he put it in his right trouser pocket. On the way back, I walked to his right, the side with the money, thinking I'd been with him all morning without getting anything for my trouble, and he'd exchanged that little book for all this money.

"I sold all the books in the house and a carpet. I knew about this passbook but didn't think it was time to use it yet. Now we have the cash, my sister and I can start our lives again. She still has three dresses and two blouses. If that's not enough, I'll get a pink one made for her. Her face is so pale, she'll look lovely and neat in a pink dress. Our uncle sent a letter saying he'd take in my sister, but I felt there was no need, and she didn't want to go. We ought to grow up together. Do you think five hundred yuan is enough for us to grow up on? We'll spend it day after day. Spending money, spending time.

"I've never seen so much money before. It should be enough to buy a whole train, one with glittering lights, just me and my sister inside. When it starts, we'll watch trees speeding past the windows, then we'll stop for a meal. We'll follow it wherever it goes. Other people can come too. We'll wait for a new era, a new beginning or else an ending.

"Five hundred yuan. I don't know how to pull off the first banknote to spend it. What would I buy? A bunch of spinach, some ground meat, or else salt and flour. In the summer should I buy a watermelon? Tomatoes might not be bad either. This money is more than the whole apartment is worth. What if someone steals it? Should I buy a popsicle for my sister? She's still plays violin, she's practicing étude number twenty-three from Kreutzer, the one that goes *do mi do mi*. Even if all her strings break, we'll have money to replace them. Or just get rid of the violin and do something else. Weave change purses out of fiberglass. Lots of girls seem to be doing that these days. I should bring her downstairs to play. Even if people curse at us for our parents being spies, so what? Hardly anyone in Ninth Building would hold that against us.

"She won't dare come downstairs. She's so timid. One night, I woke up with a shock—she was standing there. I asked what happened, she said she'd dreamed mom and dad were dead and blood had spilled on her hands. I said let them die, who asked them to be spies. When those words left my mouth, she cried, but like a grown-up, not making a sound."

When we said goodbye at the foot of the block, he didn't ask me not to say anything about the money. His trust in me made me decide to keep quiet. The next few times I went over, I admit it wasn't to view the lizards again, but to see how he was doing, if he'd bought his spinach and salt, or else violin strings. I wanted to know how he'd spent the five hundred yuan, and of course, to see his sister. Each time she stayed in her room, not making a sound. I spoke as loudly as I could, but didn't hear any movement.

She was found several months later.

When the Red Guards searched his apartment again, they discovered his long dead sister, a tiny dried-out corpse.

She was already dead the day I accompanied him to the bank, already desiccated. The grown-ups gossiping in the courtyard said a little girl's body wouldn't give off a stench.

When they took his sister away, I saw him standing by the window and remembered what he'd said that day: "Her face was blank as a mirror."

PICTURES

The bathroom wall is covered in all kinds of pictures, but I'm the only one who can see them. They were invented in my heart. I sometimes think my heart is a kind of passageway to over there, and anything that goes through, once enough time has passed, becomes almost impossible to find again.

It's not like lowering a bucket for water, and anyway I've never understood why water would flow from all over and gather itself in a well. My heart is empty, a complete blank, especially when I'm in the bathroom having a shit and the whole world seems at rest. When a heart is at rest, it concentrates only on beating, nothing else. You can't be sad while having a shit. I believe a sorrowful person wouldn't think of crapping—he hasn't the energy or the time, or simply can't squeeze anything out. A high school senior I know, Keli, was locked up for being a counter-revolutionary. When they let him out, he told everyone that for the nine days he was inside, he didn't take a single crap. Afterward, his shit came out as little black balls, painful as hell, rolling about like stones in the toilet bowl. He said he felt himself turning into a goat, tied up under the hot sun, shooting out pellets of dung. Once all the black balls were out, he felt hungry for the first time in ten days, finally revived, life returning to him. The sensation of hunger is to be cherished. He felt he should eat more, and from then on the business of each day focused on food: eating, pooping, eating some more. He said he knew then that existence wasn't eternal, because he began feeling more and more hungry, and hunger is the easiest thing to end, in whatever way. If you eat till you're full, you won't be hungry anymore. The same applies if you starve to death.

I knew him beforehand, but for some reason he became more talkative once he got out of jail. Maybe not speaking is a kind of language-hunger.

No one lets me say "taking a dump"—the grown-ups keep telling me to use "pass motion" instead. "Taking a dump" sounds rude, they say. I think this may be because "taking" is a real verb, too descriptive, and "pass motion" is a euphemism, and euphemisms are mostly polite. For instance, you can't say "How old are you?" but instead "Could I ask your year of birth?" No one ever explained this to me, but still I only say "take a dump" in my head. The phrase has a kind of glistening joy to it. Taking a dump. Quite often, I feel like calling out, "Going to take a dump!" It's not a smelly word, it contains only joy.

On the bathroom wall, a pair of glasses is pictured. Other people don't see this, but when I look at the two circles sort of next to each other—maybe someone bumped a pipe into the wall while installing it—they're obvious, though there are no eyes behind them. These aren't for someone to wear, they only exist in my mind.

And there's a lady dancing in the wind. Her tattered skirt is a scrap of paint peeling away from the wall, but most people wouldn't know how to transform this into the image of a dancing woman. If you don't look carefully, you can't do it.

There's another picture—at first I didn't know what it was, then the edges scraped away and it looked like someone's bum. When I thought that, I saw it was an invisible person sticking his bum out at me.

I shouldn't think like that.

It's not as if I can get a pencil and draw on the wall myself—nothing I draw looks like anything at all. If the world would allow one thing to be portrayed as another thing—but no, I couldn't do that either. And actually, I don't have to draw anything, nothing at all on the bathroom walls. When your heart is quiet, looking at any scratch or mark is clearer than a painting, and there's no one to disturb you. A scarred wall has life to it, and an unmarked one, a bright white wall, has none. A clean white wall has no eyes and can't see you. But a smudge is different. It knows when you're staring intently at it. It may not have eyes, but it knows. And a picture of anything, once it has senses, has life.

As Keli enthusiastically bragged about shitting goat droppings, I had a thought—what would happen if he was locked up again? Perhaps next time they let him out, his words would have grown even more, or else he'd have nothing to say at all. A person's enthusiasm for suffering is no different to his enthusiasm for good fortune. He has to speak it out loud. The first time I ate chocolate (a chunk about as big as an eraser), I felt I was tasting good fortune itself. Experiencing it for real. Because good fortune and chocolate are similar in another way—they don't last long. Even if you ate a second piece, that wouldn't make it any less short-lived.

If I went to a new bathroom, I might not see anything at all. Recognizing a picture takes a lot of time and calm contemplation before it finally leaps out at you. You stare a long while, then poof, there it is, and you wonder how you could ever have missed it. Like when you spot a faraway balloon in the vast blue sky. It looks like nothing until you spot it, then it gets bigger and bigger.

FANG YONG'S CHICKEN

Through our back window, I aimed my slingshot at Fang Yong's little rooster. The chicken abruptly arched its neck and cried out, just once. He'd only just learned to crow and the sound was odd, sending a tremor through the early morning. Fang Yong stood alone in the courtyard, the low sun stretching his shadow. He faced this elongated silhouette, as if about to fall—though if he did, it would suddenly shrink, disappearing before he actually touched it. I'd tried this experiment with some other kids, our shadows growing shorter as we plunged, joining with us at the last possible second.

I stowed my three little chicks in my pocket and went downstairs.

"Hey, have you ever eaten honeydew melon? My aunt arrived yesterday with tons of the stuff. So sweet I couldn't eat much," Fang Yong said.

"No, never. What's your aunt doing in Beijing? It's so chaotic right now."

"She got thin. Last night she kept coughing. Remember when I caught a hedgehog last year? Did you hear it cough? My aunt sounds exactly like that. I thought the hedgehog had come back. Say, what time did you wake up this morning?"

He was looking at me funny. I thought he'd guessed it was me who fired a slingshot at his chicken. Turning back, I glanced up at our back window. It was shut.

I said, "Just now."

"I was up really early. I felt like something was going to happen this morning, and it did."

Fang Yong looked different than usual.

"I know what happened." I looked at his little rooster.

He said, "You saw it too, the man. A grown-up. I didn't know him."

"It wasn't that your rooster learned to crow?"

"No." Now he looked pleased with himself, waiting for me to ask what he was talking about. I didn't ask. It was enough to know the rooster had started to crow. Best if not too many new things happen. On days when they do, I feel too overwhelmed to even have a drink of water.

"Over at Eighth Building Door Three. There's a dead person lying there." He kept his eyes on my face as he spoke. "The old lady who picks up trash saw him first. She took one look and walked away. His head was pressed against the ground. No idea how he died—there's only a little bit of blood on him."

Fang Yong pointed at the tree by Eighth Building Door Three. Sure enough, there was a body lying in its shade. I hadn't seen him from upstairs because the branches were in the way.

"Why didn't you call for a grown-up to come?"

"I've already seen five dead people, it isn't anything to get excited about. When Chen Yu's grandmother slit her throat with scissors, that was much more frightening. So much blood, it covered the whole wall, and there were even red handprints. There's nothing scary about this dead person. He looks like he's asleep. The old lady must have thought he was just having a nap, she glanced at him and walked away. Besides, my aunt's just arrived, she's coughing so much, I don't want her to get woken up by people making a fuss downstairs. Hey, did you really hear my cock crow? He doesn't sound like a chicken at all. When I first heard him, I thought some strange bird must have landed on our balcony."

"Let's wait here and see how the grown-ups look when they discover him. I want to see them scream and shout. You know what they call folk who kill themselves? Self-terminated from the People's Society. When Feng Liansong's mom died, a four-eyes shouted this at her corpse. I thought the corpse could hear but didn't care. When someone doesn't care, there's nothing you can do to them. But I think there's no need to die. If you stop feeling pain, you stop feeling anything. I like to rub in small grains of salt when I fall and hurt myself. The salt gets eaten by the pain, bit by bit. You endure it, and it feels really good afterward."

"I wonder if he killed himself. I don't think I've seen him before. He's not from Ninth Building."

More and more people were arriving. Fang Yong was surrounded by grown-ups.

Under the tree, people were staring at the dead person from some distance. The body was now covered with an old-fashioned windbreaker. Fang Yong seemed unusually excited when he spoke. He could see his aunt standing on the balcony, watching him. The grown-ups hadn't had breakfast or brushed their teeth, and bad breath swirled around their faces.

No one asked me anything, so I didn't say a word. I still hadn't walked over to take a closer look at the body.

Fang Yong's chicken, standing on the edge of the crowd, cried out again, and Fang Yong interrupted the grown-ups to shout, That's my rooster, he only started crowing this morning! No one looked at the chicken. The grown-ups walked away from Fang Yong and huddled in a group to discuss something.

As a result of their discussion, one of the grown-ups went to fetch Hong Jiong, who was in the year below me. She played the piano better than any girl I knew and was very pretty. We'd once dared each other to go stand in front of her and blow spit bubbles, but none of us could do it in the end. Thinking about it afterward, we must have been moved by her perpetual smile. We couldn't spit in that smile. It wouldn't have been a problem if she'd been laughing. Now she arrived, climbing down from the rear rack of some grown-up's bicycle, standing all alone as everyone looked at her. I didn't think she'd walk up to the body, but the grown-ups shoved her until she did, her face pale. One of them lifted a corner of the windbreaker. She looked. Everyone looked.

When she'd seen his face, she nodded to the grown-ups. She didn't cry. When she tried to walk away, the crowd moved with her, so she remained at its center. There was nowhere she could go to avoid their eyes.

I wanted to pull her away, to shield her, and then to keep her company as she cried, wiping away her tears. I'd take her hand and we'd run far, far away, the wind blowing in our faces. But I didn't do any of that. I started to hate the ice-cold body lying on the ground. He'd left too much sadness behind him. I didn't think there was anyone who could sort out the mess we were in. It was like a tangled-up bunch of string that, no matter how much you pulled, wouldn't come unknotted. And I wanted to keep pulling, even until it cut into my hands. I didn't care. Keep pulling.

There was nothing to see. I picked up my three chicks and put them back into my pocket, then went to the back courtyard.

Fang Yong was there. He said he hadn't expected it to be Hong Jiong's dad. It was only when he saw her that he started thinking how scary death was. He only felt fear when he looked at Hong Jiong's face. He asked me, Why didn't she cry, why the hell didn't she cry?

He said, They live in the East Zone. Why would her dad come all the way here, to the West Zone, to die?

I said I didn't know.

He asked, Was it because he didn't want Hong Jiong to see a dead body?

I said that might be the case.

But she saw it in the end, he said. She saw it in the end.

DOUBLE FIFTH

That winter, whenever I turned my head, I could detect the scent of my body seeping through the collar of my padded jacket, a familiar odor with no beginning or end, yet far away, farther than anything I knew or would learn in the future. This smell was a transmission of pain.

We were sweating after some roughhousing. Around that time, the taller boys could usually be persuaded to play horses, their smaller classmates mounted on their backs, forming two factions that attacked each other. The northern winter mixed sweat with wind and dirt, forming a paste that stiffened us. When I had a shower, the most immediate sensation was one of growing lighter, so weightless I felt enfeebled. A clean child seems weaker than a grubby one.

When the announcement crackled through the schoolyard warning us about meningitis, we quietened at this unfamiliar word. ". . . in the morning, rinse your mouth with saltwater. Stay away from public places . . . Long-acting sulfanilamide . . ." Fang Yong told us: Meningitis is an inflammation of the brain—that's how Double Fifth became the way he is.

Of all the disabled people I'd seen in my life, Double Fifth was the most severe. Each day as I passed by the grocery store on my way home from school, I both looked forward to and feared catching sight of him. He had superhuman strength, and mucus dripped from his nose all the way into his mouth. I'd always believed that Double Fifth lived in another world. With my own eyes, I'd seen him grabbing raw meat off a chopping board, gnawing at it as he stood in front of the counter with its display of boning knives. I often expected someone or other would come brandishing one of those knives—bleeding, screaming . . . But that never happened.

And so Double Fifth chewed his way through the red-and-white streaked meat. Even the fists landing on his head didn't distract him. We all watched him chewing on his meat. I invented the rumor that Double Fifth had a tail, and that caused us great excitement when we saw him next. Everyone felt they could make out the wolf in him.

I didn't heed the warning to rinse my mouth out with saltwater every morning. I couldn't make up my mind—did I really want to be like Double Fifth? Apart from the raw meat, I'd also seen him pee in front of a crowd. His life contained a freedom I'd never experienced. By offending every sensibility, he attracted the attention of the whole street, everyone staring at him open-mouthed. I'd never meet a disabled person with such heroism.

I thought I should await the judgment of fate, and so I skipped the saltwater and also the long-acting sulfanilamide they'd handed out. If it was my destiny to be another Double Fifth, then I would embrace it willingly, and if not I'd have no regrets.

Another of my classmates was chosen instead. He was one of the cleverest in our group. (Tunan said clever people are more likely to get brain inflammations.)

He didn't come to school for a long time. The next time we saw him, he'd become very pale and very fat. He was holding his stout grandma's hand as she gossiped with another old lady. As he listened, a string of drool trickled from his mouth, stretching thin and sticky, all the way down to the level of his heart. He hadn't become Double Fifth the way we'd imagined. Afterward, in our memories, he was fixed like that, enormously round, so large and white he might as well not have existed. During that first encounter, I had a profound realization: you can't simply become whatever you want. You might have a particular variety of disability in mind, but that may not be the type you end up turning into.

I left the city when I was almost seventeen. Later, I heard people saying Double Fifth had fallen in love with a girl who'd just started school. Each day, he stood by the gates of the elementary school as the last bell rang, and when the girl walked out he'd cry, which made him seem even more idiotic (Double Fifth was different, including the way he fell in love). Later on, the little girl transferred to another school.

Many decades have gone by now, but these people seem farther away still. I think of them again, but they've become false. I have trouble convincing myself they truly existed.

THE BAMBOO-STRAINER ANTENNA

He walked over from the other side of the building to ask if I had a rubber tube. The sun was viciously bright that day. He showed me his little finger and said about this thick. I said, Sorry, no, I used to have one, from a doctor's stethoscope, but I used it to make a sling-shot and then I lost the slingshot. He was so disappointed. I said, Maybe you can use something else, I've got a bamboo flute, key of A, with a crack in it. He said, No that won't do.

There was a dumpster nearby, beside a row of trees. We walked over to it, and he began scavenging. I wasn't sure what he was look-ing for—he discarded a Butterfly brand cigarette case and a lamp-shade with orchids on it before selecting a cracked rubber ball with a decorative print. Testing the gap with his fingers, he declared he no longer needed a length of tubing.

He mixed cornmeal and chicken feed into a thin paste, then fitted a small plastic trumpet to the crack in the ball. His family kept four chickens. He grabbed one and tied its claws together, then prized open its beak and shoved the end of the trumpet in. By squeezing the rubber, he was able to force-feed the chicken. I thought it must be ill. He said no, he'd just read in the torn pages of a book that this was how you fed Peking ducks, and he wanted to see if the same method would work on a chicken.

The thin gruel, under the pressure of the ball, mostly squirted onto his hands. Only a tiny amount actually made it into the chicken's mouth. He kept pushing regardless, wiping his hands on the bird's down. Every now and then, he stroked its crop too.

A few other kids came over, and we all squatted and stared at him. He said if he could force down half a jin of feed every day, this chicken would grow to three or four jin in about three months. Of course, a duck would be even heavier.

After the chicken died from overfeeding, he thought for a bit, then pulled a knife from his pocket. He told us chickens have two stomachs, and the one called the crop is full of sand to help digestion. He also said if we found a grain of sand in our rice we should swallow it instead of spitting it out, it'd be good for us. He cut open the chicken's crop and sure enough it was full of sand, along with the cornmeal paste he'd forced in. He thrust the knife farther along the line of its belly. We drew closer and saw the heart—like a little brown candy. I held it in my palm and said this is the only bit of flesh that can move, in fact it's still beating in my hand, you can hold it yourselves if you don't believe me. We passed it around, and everyone felt it pulsating.

He pulled out an organ from above the ribs without calling out its name, then the rest, neatly lined up on the concrete ledge. What he called the lungs were a bloody mass of bubbles.

The ants arrived soon after that.

Looking at the splayed-open chicken he said, It's just like a human body, except if you broke open the head there wouldn't be very much in here. He looked around for a stone to smash its skull, but none of us wanted to see that and we ran away.

He'd always lived with his granddad in Door Two Apartment Five, like someone living outside of time. For as long as I knew him, he'd walk past us every summer as if his head were full of weighty concerns. Once, he showed me a fragment of a Ming Dynasty inkstone and said if you fed it to a woman in childbirth it would stop the bleeding. Another time, he wrapped his teeth in the tin foil from a cigarette packet, opening wide to show everyone he met.

His whole mouth gleamed silver, and his teeth made little clanking noises when they met.

That day, the Red Guards from Middle School Number 57 searched Zhang Renhuan's home at Door One Apartment Two. Afterward, the leader stood in the archway and made a speech. He was called Zhao Qiang, from Eighth Building Door Two, three years older than me. As he spoke, we stared at his gun belt—a genuine gun belt—which had five stars and "August 1st" carved on its metal clasp. I dreamed about owning a belt like that, one you could raise up into the air and lash out at someone with. A belt for hitting people. I stared at that gun belt for quite a while, entranced.

Zhang Renhuan's home was now full of broken objects. Her granny was kneeling on a pile of broken glass, muttering something under her breath. Her dad stood, head lowered, on a stool that kept wobbling back and forth. Her smallest brother ran in and out of the room, looking excited at what was going on.

A female Red Guard grabbed my shirt collar from behind. Her age was somewhere in between my two older sisters, and her eyes were very narrow. She asked what my background was, looking ready to hit me. I said I didn't know. She asked which building I was from. I said Ninth Building. She said, You stinking bastard intellectual, I'll give you one chance—go kick over that stool.

I got ready to obey her instructions. This was nothing to me. I'd already smashed all the glass panes in the principal's office with a stone. My only worry was that when the stool tumbled over, Zhang Renhuan's dad might land on me.

At that moment, *he* appeared at the entrance to Door Two, with a long bamboo pole strapped around his waist. Atop the pole was a broken bamboo strainer with metal mesh, to which was affixed a wire that ran down to the crystal radio receiver in his hand. A pair of black headphones was clasped over his ears. He walked over to the crowd, still fiddling with the tuning knob.

Zhao Qiang paused in his speech to watch him, and so did the rest of us. I didn't know what he was listening to, but some kind of sound was coming over the thing. I was fascinated by that antenna reaching up so high, the ingenuity of the bamboo strainer as a receiver. It reminded me of the spider web aerial I'd seen in books. I walked over and asked if he could really hear something. He said yes, only the station wasn't very clear. He plucked off the headphones and let me put them on. I heard a group of people singing, then someone discussing society. He said the wire wasn't coiled properly because it had been spliced too many times, and also the air capacitor was too small, which slowed it down. (I'd made a crystal radio receiver once. My antenna ran along the window, grounded along the hot water pipe.)

When the metal clasp lashed through the air between us, I felt I'd been wrong in my admiration for that gun belt. It would never belong to me.

*

The two of us stepped into the courtyard at the same time early the next morning, our heads wrapped in two different types of bandages. On such mornings, the yard seemed to fill with a kind of mournful heroism. We'd both become the focal point of the group.

He walked over and said to me, Those round things between the chicken's ribs yesterday, those were its testicles. A rooster's balls grow inside its abdominal cavity. I didn't know what testicles were, so he grabbed his own crotch, clutching it earnestly. I immediately said I understood. This was the first time I had a sense of the seriousness and self-sacrifice required by scholarship.

Neither of us had anything further to say about testicles. I asked, What's your background? He adjusted his bandages, pressed the bruise on his cheekbone, and answered, Martyr.

SPRINGTIME

1.

Yao Nan removed the stuffing from his quilted jacket. He'd found a little sparrow, so young it hadn't yet sprouted any down or opened its eyes. The tiny thing was warmer than anyone's palm. It opened its mouth, shaking its head back and forth, but we didn't know what to do.

Springtime makes you feel at a loss—it's uncomfortable whether you keep your windows shut or have them open. We stood around in the courtyard waiting for the spring-chick vendor.

The night before, I'd soaked my hands in warm water then scrubbed them pale, rubbing clam lotion into every crack and fold. Now they were firmly stuffed into my trouser pockets. Washing my hands seemed to make them lighter; a pair of clean hands has no energy.

Yao Nan said, Every year it only feels like spring when we come to tomb-sweeping time. He could never understand why we'd wait for springtime, when flowers were blooming, to visit the dead and sing those mournful songs. Spring passed by so quickly, it seemed over as soon as we were done tending to the graves.

The flesh-bird slept in his hands.

Yao Nan said, Why do we have tomb-sweeping before spring-outing? A large part of his year was spent waiting for spring-outing time. He'd go anywhere. The night before, he'd often be unable to sleep, his schoolbag packed with bread and a water bottle placed at the head of his bed, having nightmares about waking up late and missing the spring-outing bus, standing alone at the meeting place, crying. The conclusion of this dream always made him determined to leave this city and the people in it. He felt so put-upon.

The little flesh-bird had old-looking skin, greenish and wrinkled. If we nudged it onto its back, we could see its belly rise and fall. It was breathing. Newly-hatched birds are old and ugly, growing slowly into the appearance of a bird, just as human babies look like old men when they're just born. If you were to fling this bird into the air, it would fall and shatter like a clod of earth.

Why not throw it? When it actually does die, it won't shatter like that.

Yao Nan said that year's grave-sweeping was the most fun. So many tombs had been pushed over, some marked with a big black cross. They didn't sing the usual songs. He saw someone's gravestone scrawled over with the words: *This person diddled women and died, serves him right.* I said, I saw that too. He replied, It doesn't matter what you write, he's dead anyway, he doesn't know, you could sing to him or scold him, he still wouldn't know. If I died, I'd bury myself in a secret place, like missing spring-outing, dying alone, escaping far from here.

The flesh-bird opened its mouth wide again, thrusting its head out. I said, Think of a way to feed it. Yao Nan opened his mouth and put the bird in, so it could suck at his saliva.

Yao Nan said, If not for the spring-outing, there'd be no spring-time at all. If "spring" was just a word, no matter who gave it to me, I wouldn't take it. Why would I want something I can't see or touch? Think about it—a blind man's sensation of spring might be only the clothes he removes from his body, the warmth he feels, but warmth won't change his dead eyes, he can't see the flowers, even if he were to touch a pink peach blossom, its petals would feel no different than vegetable peelings. If you gave you him vegetable peel and told him it was peach blossom, could he imagine the flower and the springtime? Why not give him a light bulb, one that's still warm, and the heat might bring some light into the darkness of his heart—don't you feel that when enduring a burn, your heart lightens? If I could, I'd give him a light bulb, and tell him it was spring. That might give him a clearer image than the flowers.

I don't like peach blossoms. When they fall and get wet with rain, they seem especially dirty. If not for these flowers, I wouldn't feel the rain was dirty.

The flesh-bird wanted more of Yao Nan's saliva. He fished out half a bun from his pocket, stale and black, pinched a piece off, chewed it, and held the bird's beak to his mouth. It ate with gusto, throat quivering. I thought we may be able to raise this sparrow after all.

Yao Nan said, If we went on the spring-outing and then stopped classes, I'd be so happy—but I wouldn't want school to be cancelled if it meant no spring-outing. Time moves faster in the spring. Didn't you see the pagoda blossoms are already out? We bring springtime back with us from the graveyard. I want something different, I want to change it for the spring that comes off the lake, the green grass, the wet soil. I'd even write a whole essay about springtime—you all know how good my essays are, didn't one get read out in your class? The trick is not to write the way the teacher says. My essays make the teacher forget all his words. They say I have imagination, but I think everyone has that, they just don't dare to use it. But if you didn't give me springtime, I wouldn't be willing to think either, I'd refuse to imagine anything. How pointless a springtime without thought would be. Do you know what I mean when I say "pointless"? Pointless is this afternoon, me standing here, you watching me feed a little knob of flesh.

In the end we agreed that the next day we'd walk to Beihai

Park—we'd make our own spring-outing. Me, Yao Nan, Little Jianzi, Tunan, Dingzi, and the flesh-bird.

Spring was the same as always. When you enter a new spring-time, the first thing you think of is bygone ones, never mind which year, springtimes that have slipped away.

Beihai was the same as always, but as soon as we walked in, our breath grew carefree.

We didn't have enough money to rent a boat, not even for the deposit. We watched other people rowing across the lake and felt as if their springtime held something more than ours.

Everyone's springtime is different.

We concentrated hard by Five Dragons Pavilion, trying to see ourselves clearly in the water. We didn't look like we'd imagined—we weren't wearing new clothes, hadn't put on neckerchiefs, and some of us needed a haircut. This wasn't a school-organized spring-outing, it was less anxious. We felt this liberty and gazed freely at ourselves upside-down in the water.

Tunan ate pagoda flowers in handfuls. He cinched his belt around his waist, then climbed up and stuffed blossoms into his undershirt so it swelled, and the rest of us ate from his chest too, even though they stank of his sweat.

As we walked through the park and began to relax, I thought of what Yao Nan said the day before, the word "pointless." Saying this word made me feel grown up. In front of Nine Dragon Wall, I suddenly blurted out, "Pointless!" The others—as well as two passersby who were taking photographs—turned back to look at me, startled. I couldn't resist laughing out loud, pointing at the dragons, shouting out "Pointless!" And then we were all running in the spring wind and calling out, "Pointless!" We climbed up the white tower to stare at the boats on the lake which seemed motionless; we looked down at the tiny cars and people and felt we were giants, pronouncing all of them pointless. How bright that word sounded, how far it spread that spring day.

2.

By the time we walked back to Ninth Building that day, the willow
wreaths around our heads had withered, but no one could bear to
get rid of theirs. We wanted to walk into the courtyard still wearing
our wreaths, so everyone could see we'd returned from the spring,
we'd been on our spring-outing—to Beihai. We were very tired, a
springtime exhaustion.

We walked instead of taking the bus, and spent our fares on pop-
sicles, which gave off vapor in the hot air. Each of us dedicated himself
to his treat, walking as we ate. As we passed Guangji Temple, through
a crack in the door we could see several monks burning books. We
watched for a while, but the flames didn't look good by daylight.

In a hutong, we saw a child with convulsion sickness sitting by
a courtyard entrance, his left hand hooked toward his chest, trembling, dribbling out the right side of his mouth. The doorways in
that courtyard were black holes, the sunlight dazzling around them.
The child was about our age, yet blue veins stood out on his forehead
and face. The five of us stood in a row to stare at him, his hand like
a metal hook and the sticky, oozing saliva. We watched with great
concentration. After some time, he shouted something at us, using a
lot of effort, but we still couldn't make out what. He drooled more,
faster, as he scolded us.

The five of us, wearing our willow wreaths, walked through many
similar streets. We weren't familiar with this area. Ninth Building
was in the rural part of this city, surrounded by vegetable fields and
farming folk who ate whatever they gathered. They'd split open a
huge eggplant, chewing its flesh, dark faces bobbing against white
pith. They snorted noisily and spat onto the greenery. When we
stared at them, they flung eggplant skins at us. If it was time to water
the crops, they'd rest their chins on the handles of their spades, and
shout across the distance at each other. We felt their speech had a lot
of meaningless passion.

It was evening by the time we arrived back at Ninth Building. Entering the courtyard, we saw Wang Dayi forcing Zhang Liang's granny from Door One to clamber onto a cement ping pong table. With braided willow branches, fresher than the ones around our heads, he was whipping the old lady. Small children circled them, watching, shouting, "Defeat the landlord curs!" No one noticed the willow wreaths we wore still had a green fragrance.

Wang Dayi made Granny Zhang crawl like a dog on the table. Her bound feet flopped about, looking ridiculously tiny and clumsy. We heard her wide cotton trousers chafing against the concrete surface. Wang Dayi lashed her with the willow whip and shouted at her to go faster.

She turned over and sat on the table. "Children, Granny's tired."

"Defeat the landlord curs!"

Her gray hair fluttered, shaken by the shouting.

As she started crawling again, I wondered if I could call her Granny Zhang in the future. She once washed some tomatoes for me, three of them. As I ate, her toothless mouth moved incessantly, and I felt she was asking me to taste a tomato on her behalf, a bright red one that begged to be eaten.

Now her mouth moved again as she said, "You might as well let me die."

Wang Dayi beat her with springtime willow branches.

Plumes of earth rose into the air.

The five of us split up. Little Jianzi—whose father was a revolutionary cadre—ripped the willow branch off his head and squeezed eagerly into the crowd. He felt that whipping Granny Zhang was a correct activity, or else a proof of his identity. As he raised his lash, I thought of the mouth we'd seen on our way back, dribbling saliva as it scolded us. That mouth wasn't mine.

Ninth Building had many windows. Each now contained a grown-up's face. Some held two. They all looked like they didn't quite dare to watch. All the windows remained shut.

As Little Jianzi re-braided his willow whip and raised it high, a window opened on the second story of Door Two. His mother, a young and very pretty woman, shouted, "Little Jianzi, come inside!" He said, "I want to keep playing." She called, "Come home!" in a calm voice, not too loud, but all the children turned to look at her. It was an ice-cold sound, not resonant, quietly determined. Little Jianzi threw aside his willow branch and wriggled out of the group. He was only in Year Three, and we were quite good friends. Earlier that day, he'd bought me a popsicle.

Several windows opened now, and grown-ups called their children's names. Dinnertime.

I went home too. From the Door Four stairwell, I saw Wang Dayi wielding a pair of scissors, cutting off Granny Zhang's hair. She sat on the dirty ping pong table, hanks of white hair tumbling down all around her. I plucked the willow wreath off my head and flung it to the ground.

I walked up the stairs, inhaling along the way aromas from the various kitchens: onions and eggs.

ILLNESS

The only time a grown-up touched our skin was when we had a fever. They'd press their foreheads to ours, trying to see whose was hotter.

When I was ill, I had to take pills.

The hardest pills to swallow were licorice ones. They had a sweet taste from the medicine itself, a deceptive sweetness. Medicine ought to be bitter, like goldthread pills. When you place one of those on your tongue, bitterness fills your whole body.

That morning, I could see my veins throbbing. When I lifted my arms, a tendon in my wrist moved up and down *puh-duh puh-duh*, the only part of my body that wasn't still. It moved even when you slept, when you were thinking, when you were silent, moving so stealthily you heard nothing, no sound, but still it pulsed, and when you looked at it you felt you'd never had any control over your own body—were you really yourself? At best you were incomplete, not a whole self, since so many parts of you lay beyond your control.

He said he had septicemia. When a person told someone else he was living with some kind of illness, the word that came most easily to mind was "philosophy." I didn't know what philosophy was—I'd heard the word but didn't know its meaning. Still, it felt as if a person trying to explain what afflicted his body must have something to do with philosophy.

At the time I said, So in the future you'll be able to study philosophy.

He thought for a while about my words. I felt his thoughts reaching far away, not in time but into a distance, like the word "freedom," impossible to interrupt and impossible to attain.

He held on to the word "philosophy" and we began to play with magnetic strips. We'd stolen these from the subway construction site. The grown-ups called these things "mosaics" but it felt a bit pretentious when I did that. Instead, we called them "magnets," using our own language to protect ourselves. For instance, we called our schoolbags "shit shovels," Old Sun the doorman was "Old Pipe," and banknotes were "leaves." Police officers were "landmines." When these nouns popped out of our mouths, our world felt different to the one the grown-ups lived in, and this sensation was the pillar that propped up our universe, enabling us to live sincerely and passionately.

We played "drop one" or "drop two," which was harder than "grab all." The aim was to transfer a row of magnets from the palm to the back of the hand, allowing just one or two to drop in the instant you flipped them back into your grasp. This was a trick we'd developed with arduous practice. Apart from our own language, we also developed a number of skills the grown-ups said were useless. As well as the magnet game, there were also marbles, flying sticks, throwing knives. This was how we sustained ourselves. I don't mean individually, but as a group of children.

He played well, winning several rounds. A sick person is better able to stay focused.

Apart from winning and losing at magnets, we also exchanged a pair of words that day: septicemia and philosophy. I must confess his word had more of an influence on me. To my mind, he wasn't a regular sick person—he had no fever, no running nose, no bandages. If his face hadn't been so pale, I might not have thought he was ill at all. That's why I thought septicemia must have something in common with the word "philosophy." Both were empty, unattainable, only seeming to exist when you named them.

That afternoon, I found a little respect and admiration for a kid with septicemia. Think about it, it happened to him and not someone else—not me, not a grown-up. This was special, I had to admit. He arrived in our midst with the glory of septicemia, definitely a reason for solemnity. I felt I ought to lose to him at magnets as a token of esteem.

Wang Dazhi appeared wearing his older brother's armband just as I was losing my final magnet. He walked over from Door One, like a shadow accompanying the Red Guard insignia on his right arm, trying to force us into being his audience. When his eyes landed on us, his heart was thumping away on that armband. I could tell his right arm had grown heavy, a constant flash of red in his peripheral vision. A fresh, unfamiliar sensation of honor—for honor must always be fresh and unfamiliar.

As these thoughts passed through me, the sick boy felt them too.

He pulled from his pocket first the stack of magnets, then a little bottle, from which he shook out some white pills. These he shoved into his mouth with grubby fingers, like eating a handful of beans. I said, Did you swallow? He said yes and opened his mouth to show me.

I suddenly wanted to take a pill too, or to gulp down my medicine like he did. There was nothing wrong with me, but I wanted to take something just then. I asked if it was bitter. He said no, tasteless. I thought he wasn't making enough effort with his answers. Medicine couldn't possibly have no taste.

I said, Give me a pill to try. He said fine. The bottle came out again and he let one tablet spill out for me. Just like him, I tossed it into my mouth and flung my head back, trying to swallow. Nothing—it wouldn't go down. But I could taste its lack of bitterness. In fact, there was a sweetness to it. I said, This pill is sweet, how strange that medicine should be sweet.

Wang Dazhi raised his arm even higher, glaring at us.

He put the pill bottle away and said, This kind of medicine is sugar-coated, but when it reaches your stomach, it'll feel uncomfortable, you'll burp as if you've eaten limescale. Whenever this kind of belch rose from his belly, his insides felt like a pot of water, growing hotter day and night but never reaching boiling point, accumulating layer after layer of limescale like the aluminum kettle in his house, getting heavier and heavier until one day he'd be unable to move, and then he'd be dead. Neither of you have felt this, he said, That's what illness is.

Wang Dazhi lowered his arm. His right hand crept behind him and scratched his ass.

I said, You should definitely study philosophy. He asked why. I said, Philosophy and septicemia go well together.

He didn't say anything for a while.

He said he'd wanted to play military parts in operas, the kind where you stand on stage in thick-soled boots waving a saber around, turning a somersault or two, lying absolutely straight to play dead, not bending your body at all, an even more touching sight than an actual death, falling to the ground with a thud.

He wasn't scared of the word "death" and didn't fear falling down and lying absolutely straight. When he demonstrated, the magnets fell from his pocket and scattered over the floor. As Wang Dazhi knelt to help, he asked what philosophy was. Dazhi scooped up the magnets with his right hand, as if his arm were bare.

He stood up and said, Philosophy is studying things to do with life and death, and also with the heavens and earth, and also with people.

I hadn't guessed this might be the meaning, but maybe he was right. When he'd finished explaining, I felt this was the philosophy I'd thought about deep down. But if he hadn't said it like that, I'd never have found these words for myself. Living in this world, there were many words I hadn't been able to say. He taught me many things that day. This was the first time I'd lost so many magnets without minding.

A belch escaped from him. He said to me, I burped, see if you can smell the limescale. I took a step closer and said I could. Septicemia seemed more real to me just then.

He didn't ask Wang Dazhi to smell. He said, I have another type of medicine at home, sour and bitter, do you want to try? I said yes. He said, Come with me then.

The magnets in his pocket clicked together as he walked. I followed him. Behind us, Wang Dazhi called out, "Wait for me! I'm coming too."

I LOVE XI XIAOMEI

This is the shutter, this is the lens, this is the viewfinder, horizontal or vertical. If you want to load more film, pull this lever to open it up. It's black inside, and if you don't click the shutter it remains black always, black as night, you know, like the expression "endless night." Like your tomb after you're dead. The shutter lets in an instant of light—*ka-tscha!*—and an image blossoms on the film, a person or a tree. Photographs are shadows left behind by grave robbers.

Dr. Shi once posed for nude photos. She was young then, and this was in the old society, taken with a camera. To make an old woman look at pictures of her naked younger body—that's the greatest tragedy. In *Dream of the Red Chamber*, the tragedy isn't young Lin Daiyu dying of tuberculosis—it would only be tragic if she lived to be as old as Dowager Jia. All the sad stories I know are connected with youth and beauty. What? If you don't know what "nude" means, what are you doing playing around with a camera? It means naked. Bare-assed. The only thing I don't understand is why Dr. Shi held on to these pictures. For herself to look at, or other people? She's an old woman now, who would she show them to?

When she bared her body back then, apart from the camera taking her in, there must also have been at least one pair of eyes, whoever took the photo. Did they belong to a man or a woman? I heard her husband was mayor of Hangzhou when it was occupied by the Japanese. It's hard to imagine that a person who posed for nude pictures could also be a doctor. These two ideas don't go together.

She once examined me when I was ill, her ice-cold stethoscope pressing against my back and chest. She asked me to open my mouth and briskly flicked back my eyelids. She thought I might have brain inflammation.

*

After my older brother finished talking about Dr. Shi, he handed the camera to me. It only takes 110 film, he said, You can't find that anywhere these days, so it's basically trash, old and obsolete. It can't see any longer.

It didn't matter to me that there wasn't any film. I'd seen grown-ups using a camera—as long as you pressed the button, everything would be captured.

Xi Xiaomei was standing by the lime pond as I walked past, staring intently at the lime frothing into bubbles. A chunk of fresh lime opens like a fist when it touches water. I'd seen this, the white gas and sizzle it emits. If you stuck your hand into the water, it'd feel as if it had been scalded for a few days afterward. She was exhilarated when she called to me, asking me to come closer to look at the blister on her toe, clear and shiny, the size of a date.

"I have hives. It's an allergy, I'm not infectious," she said. "Do you want to touch my blister? It's fine as long as you don't burst it."

I knelt down and carefully ran my finger around the little bubble so gently I hardly felt it. She said, "I was so worried I'd pop it last night, I tied my legs together before I went to sleep. I want to see how big it'll grow. If it gets to the size of a walnut, the liquid inside will slosh around when I walk, like a rattle. I haven't thought about anything else for the last few days. I've already shown it to seven people today, but they didn't get to touch, I was afraid it'd burst. You're the first one. Before you showed up, I was sure you'd walk by any minute."

It suddenly seemed to me that if the need arose, I'd be willing to fight for Xi Xiaomei. Dingzi once told me she'd given him three Imperial Concubine candy wrappers. I felt as if he'd sullied something. The finger that had touched her blister now felt weighed down.

That morning, I stood with Xi Xiaomei by the lime pond. We talked about nothing in particular. Springtime began that day with that blister, that little bump called hives.

In the summer, she wore a pair of pink flip-flops and her hair was darker than usual. She sat in front of me in class. The teacher had assigned me to recite "Lesson Eight: The Story of Yang Jingyu," but I hadn't managed to memorize this passage the day before. Learning lines wasn't something I enjoyed—when I'd read something, I didn't want to go back and look at it a second time. I was about to confess when Xi Xiaomei laid her textbook open on the corner of her desk, pushing her black hair aside so I could see. I began reciting, glimpsing the words out of the corner of my eye. My voice was strong and resonant.

I hadn't asked her to do this, and she never spoke of it again. Having been part of this conspiracy gave me a strange sensation. Like she was not just a classmate, but a relative too. Her family lived at Ninth Building Door One. I often saw her dad and granny around. They spoke Shanghainese when it was just them. Hearing the family talk Shanghainese as they walked down the street felt like watching a black and white film, *Ten Thousand Lights* or something. Her dad had a few pairs of shiny leather shoes, and his trousers weren't the usual black or dark blue, but coffee colored. He was an interpreter. Once I saw him in his coffee-colored trousers talking to a Russian expert, his high voice floating on top of the Russian's laughter. I don't remember him speaking much Mandarin. Even his laugh only appeared when he spoke a foreign language, as if it had nothing at all to do with his family, Ninth Building, the Design Institute, or Xi Xiaomei. He seemed alone, completely isolated among the grown-ups of Ninth Building, friendless. He didn't join in the Sunday communal cleaning up.

I never visited their home. Whenever I called for her, she'd run outside immediately, sometimes still clutching a pencil. She kept her candy wrappers in an old textbook. I had more, but hers were flatter and in better condition. She said she washed them and dried them in the sun before pressing them, so there wasn't any lingering tackiness.

Pretending I didn't want any more candy wrappers, I allowed her to pick any of mine she liked. Within her enthusiasm lingered a little shyness, which again put me in mind of *Dream of the Red Chamber*. I traded away wrapper after wrapper for her facial expressions, looking solemn while waves of joy passed through my body. For a few days I went through neighboring trash cans looking for more wrappers, discovering rare complete sets of *Mickey Mouse* and *Big White Rabbit*. I didn't bring these to her straight from the garbage. For her sake, I washed them first, with as much care and attention as when I'd stroked her blister. I never asked myself why I was doing this, whether it was because I'd fallen for her. I didn't know how to ask such questions back then, my only purpose was to make her happy.

Some of the other kids began to talk about me, calling me a pervert. One day I got home to find "Big Zou and Little Xi getting married" scrawled across the Door Four corridor in Fang Yong's handwriting. These words didn't make me angry. I didn't know whether someone had written the same thing at Door One. I didn't give her any candy wrappers that day. Instead, I lured her out with a three-cornered stamp, taking the opportunity to look into her eyes to see if anything had changed. It hadn't. If anything, she seemed even happier than usual, and I repeated silently in my heart "Big Zou and Little Xi getting married." I almost said the words aloud. Before they could slip out, I ran away.

That evening, the happiness faded as I began to regret she hadn't seen the graffiti, and even considered sneaking out in the small hours to copy the words onto the wall by Door One. I wanted to know how she'd react. Back then, I didn't know anything, had no idea what getting married really meant, but I felt that if we kept trading candy wrappers day after day, it would lead inevitably to marriage.

Dingzi told me Xi Xiaomei's family was being transferred to the Zhongtiao Mountains. I didn't believe him at first. He said, "Her dad committed an error. When he went abroad with Director Li, they took part in independent activity one night. That's an incorrect action. Her dad, and also Tongge's dad, will be sent to the mines in the Zhongtiao Mountains."

I had no impression of those mountains. It seemed impossible that she could leave—she lived at Door One, which was her home, and I was at Door Four. This state of affairs felt eternal. Even after she told me herself she had to go, I had no way of imagining life without her.

She told me that when she heard the news, she wasn't sad at all. They'd have to take a train all the way through Hebei Province into Henan. It was all mining hills there. She asked if I'd ever been to the mountains. I said no, but perhaps there'd be interesting wild animals there, and hunters too. She said yes, she'd looked at a map and it was string after string of hills. She ran back home to get the map to show me. Everywhere she pointed to was reddish-brown, making me think of her dad's coffee-colored trousers.

I couldn't think of a way to say goodbye. Finally, I decided to photograph her. It didn't matter that there was no film in the camera, the important thing was the process of taking a girl's picture. A ritual, a way of saying farewell. Anyway, I didn't understand why you needed film to make a photograph. I was only in fourth grade and we hadn't learned the word "negatives" yet.

When I went to look for her with my camera, she was thrilled and told me to wait a moment while she changed her dress.

That summer afternoon, I took Xi Xiaomei's photograph by August First Lake. Her smile was brighter than the sun, and I pulled it over and over again into the black box, which was connected to my heart. Again and again I clicked the shutter, *ka-tscha! ka-tscha!* We put together a collection of pictures that knew no boundaries. When it came to evening, she said, Could we take one together? I said of course, and we asked an older girl passing by to take one of us by the lake. We stood side by side, and her hand reached for mine. My heart became suddenly chaotic, and the smile I summoned for the camera grew into a kind of sorrow. She was going to leave, departing for those reddish-brown hills. The reality of her absence began that moment.

I thought she should display sadness too, but she never did, she was too excited about the train ride and those mountains. Soon after our day with the camera, Xi Xiaomei vanished.

Her family departed in a great hurry. One afternoon, I looked in their window and the apartment was completely empty.

I still believed I could get photographs out of the camera. When I opened the casing at the back, I didn't see the pictures I'd hoped for. In fact, it contained nothing at all. My brother said, How could you get photos without putting film in? I still didn't know what "film" was. But it didn't matter, I recalled every image perfectly. I could see her anytime I wanted.

A couple of winters later, I got a letter from her. It was a dark evening. I sat in my room on the fourth floor reading it as a wild wind howled outside.

My dear Didi, How are you?

My family has lived in the Zhongtiao Mountains for more than a year now. I've graduated from elementary school now, have you?

Things are bad here. There are no wild animals, and no hunters either. Pigs and dogs roam the streets. It's filthy. When it rains, there's mud everywhere, even in the bathrooms. I see maggots squirming in it. The night we arrived, I cried. From the first moment, I wanted to go back to Beijing. I missed our classmates and wrote you a letter, but tore it up instead of mailing it.

More and more, I'm starting to feel as if none of you care about me any longer. I'm all alone here. I don't understand the dialect they speak and don't dare to wear dresses when I go out, not even in summer. Every morning and evening, I stick my head through the window to look at the sky. At first, I felt like this place was a nightmare and tried to make myself wake up and return to Beijing, to Ninth Building. Now it seems like Beijing was the dream, along with everything that happened before. My accent is starting to change. I sometimes use Beijing dialect at school, but not outside. I don't know how this happened. After I left the city, I realized for the first time what sadness was. I wrote in my journal every day, trying to remember my previous life. I think I've stopped growing up and started growing old. I miss all of you, but I keep it to myself. I'm happiest when I think about you, but I know I'll never see you again. There used to be a hornet nest on our balcony. I'd see them flying back and forth. Then one day someone smashed it, and I saw the hornets come home, just hovering there and buzzing helplessly. I wondered why they were still there—why they didn't just fly away and build a new nest somewhere else? How foolish I was then.

Do you still collect candy wrappers? It's been a long time since I opened the textbook I keep mine in. Every time I want to look at them, my tears start flowing, and I don't want to let the grown-ups see me cry. I know they watch me in the dark. Why do they feel so guilty about me?

I've finally come to terms with it. I couldn't have stayed alone in Beijing, I'm still a child, and have to go where my parents go. I'm getting used to life here. Yesterday, I got into a fight with a bigger girl. I yelled at her in the local dialect—I no longer swear like a Beijinger. The words won't come out. But each time I curse the local way, I move farther from how I used to be. I've only just graduated elementary school, I have no idea what's going to happen to me in the future.

I've written about a big jumble of things, but you mustn't worry about me. I was going to tear this letter up, then I remembered I wanted to ask you about those pictures we took by August First Lake. I want very much to see them, I don't know why. A strong wind is blowing outside, it's going to snow soon. I want to see those photographs. I miss you very much. I've always thought of you as my older brother, or someone even closer than a brother.

That's enough, I'm going to mail this now. I hope I don't chicken out on my way to the post office.

Xi Xiaomei
October 30, 1966

I began to cry, not knowing what to do. There weren't any photographs. I wanted to write back to her but didn't know how to explain. In the middle of the night, I pulled open the camera, but there had been no miracle, it was still empty. My dad had been locked up in the cowshed by that time, and our house felt cold and empty. I realized nothing could be done about what had already happened.

The next day, I walked past her window again. A new family had moved in. They had a chubby little daughter who talked funny, with some kind of accent.

As I walked past the Door One passageway, I could still see the words on the wall. "Big Zou and Little Xi getting married." With my hand, I wiped the words away, flakes of whitewash drifting away as I rubbed.

The words went to a distant place, where it was surely snowing.

CHICKEN BLOOD

There is too much to think about in the summer. All the different summers gone by.

I once got into an argument with a kid from my building about whether you felt more refreshed after a hot or cold shower. We didn't reach a conclusion.

As far back as I could remember, my dad had taken cold baths in all seasons. Even on the coldest winter day, he'd lower himself into a bath leaving only his nose and mouth above the water, teeth chattering. After about fifteen minutes he'd pull himself out and rub himself red with a towel. The whole process seemed tragic yet joyful. He encouraged me to try it once, but my experience was neither tragic nor joyful. It just felt like I was making life difficult for myself.

My dad jumped on whatever health fad was in the air. During the Three Years of Disaster, it was fashionable to brew ball-algae, so he did; then it was kombucha, arm-swinging calisthenics, crushed Sichuan peppercorns, plum blossom kung fu, eight-brocade qigong. In his eighties, he could still write calligraphy with big or small brushstrokes, or carry a basket of vegetables more than a li. The reason for this longevity must be his passion and faith in life.

During the Cultural Revolution, chicken blood injections were the latest thing. There'd always be a line at the public clinic, people clutching live chickens and waiting for the nurses—perspiring from their running around—to lift the bird's wing, find a vein, rub on iodine, and stick a needle in. The startled fowl would shut its eyes in confusion. After a moment, its blood would flow into the veins of its human owner. After this humanitarian sacrifice, the chicken stood unsteadily on the ground, puzzled: Where's the fire, where's the pot, why haven't these people slaughtered, plucked and eaten me? What are they playing at? Is blood thicker than soup?

What about the person who now had chicken blood flowing in their veins? Weren't they afraid they'd one day be seized by an urge to run onto the balcony and start crowing?

I was afraid. I had a rooster at home who brought me a lot of glory in our courtyard cockfights. He was a big hero, and I didn't want his blood to find its way into a regular person's body by underhand methods (not that I'd never thought of my dad as a regular person, but it was even more important to protect my noble bird's hot blood and lofty spirit). Roosters were becoming harder to find in the market, and I started to wonder if half the people I passed in the street had had chicken blood infusions. They were all grownups. Children love chickens more but would never think of having anything to do with their blood.

While I was at school, our neighbors took my rooster. One time only, they said, Xu Feng's dad had chronic diarrhea. I came home to find him slumped in his coop, light as a sheet of paper, trembling all over. Lifting his wing, I found a yellow iodine stain. His heroic blood had been stolen to cure chronic diarrhea. He no longer greeted the dawn, nor was he as fearless on the battlefield. Our courtyard cockfights became more about nursing these weak roosters back to health, the great heroes destroyed by the grown-ups.

I asked Xu Feng if his father's diarrhea was better. He said not particularly. Instead, he had a new illness: bad temper. His dad never used to hit him, but after the infusion, he got angry over a small matter, something about peeling a radish, and lashed out at him with a chopper. Your rooster must be too powerful, said Xu Feng. Perhaps,

I said. Why not use hen's blood, then everyone will become gentler? No, only rooster blood has Revolutionary spirit, otherwise where will people get the energy to overturn the old society? But not everyone is suited to receiving an injection. If my dad had one, he'd be the one waving a chopper.

I vividly remember the two of us analyzing the implications of chicken blood injections.

At some point, everyone stopped having these infusions. I never heard anyone say it was harmful, it just became unfashionable all of a sudden.

They said on the radio that a chicken is ready for slaughter at seven months, by which time it'd have consumed fifty jin of feed and could fetch a market price of about six yuan.

So now chickens would only be used as food—how much lonelier for both them and us.

YANGFANGDIAN

The district we lived in was called Yangfangdian. I'd never bothered to find out where this name came from—it seemed like a foolish question. There were some place names I didn't like much, and plenty I outright hated. Those names had been acquired before you got there and wouldn't change after you arrived, plus you had no idea where the names came from or how much longer they'd continue being used. You had to live on that name, like a guest. "I live in Yangfangdian." Think about it—Yangfangdian doesn't care that you live there, it's indifferent whether you stay or go. Ninth Building was different. As soon as it was built, you arrived. The freshly-painted walls gave you hives. Some of the marks now scarring the building were left by you. Its scent and appearance were connected to you.

The day Big Qi arrived with the news, we were immersed in our game of donkey-riding. It was winter, and we could all smell our own perspiration but oddly enough no one else's. The winter was too cold and the scent of sweat too precious. You'd occasionally lower your head and the odor rose from your shirt collar, a kind of knowing warmth, your own, impossible to explain, unknowable by anyone else.

Big Qi said, This afternoon they dug up the princess's grave. The subway tunnel was supposed to go through there, so they went ahead and dug it up. They found all kinds of things. Bolts of silk and precious jewels. The cloth was still vivid when they pulled it out, gold and silver threads like opera costumes, but in a short while they all faded, just a bit of sun and wind, and the colors fell away like crushed flower petals. Everyone stood frozen. They didn't dare to move, as if hands that had touched the fabric would also crumble.

When they opened the princess's coffin, the wind stopped and a glow emanated from the ground. The princess had a pale face, delicate as jade, and fragrance wafted from her. Her eyes had never shut but were narrowed in a half-smile. The workers and foremen refused to do any more—they didn't know how to proceed. The princess was still lying in her coffin.

By the time he'd finished telling us, the sky was dark and it was time to go home for dinner. Instead, the seven of us clambered over the western wall of Ninth Building and ran along the narrow road to the princess's tomb—the neighborhood, about two kilometers from Ninth Building, was actually called Princess's Tomb, Gongzhufen.

In the dark, seven pairs of cotton shoes pounded the dirt road like a regiment on the move. None of us spoke. Everyone held onto their own imagined picture of the princess. To seek an audience with a princess on a winter's night just as the stars appeared—what could be more enchanting? The princess might be dead—truly dead, not make-believe—but she was still a princess after all! Where there's a princess, there'll be a story. If this tale had a place for us, we'd go to a different world, one created out of words, where ordinary people couldn't enter, and in this place the story would be enacted again and again, each time you brought it to mind it'd happen in front of you, and generation after generation would do this without getting tired of it. Neither side would get bored. I wanted nothing more than to enter a story, one told by a toothless old lady or a blind man in dark glasses. It didn't matter who was telling it as long as I could go in.

Hopefully the princess wouldn't have decayed like those bolts of cloth. What would she change into, fragments of white jade? A porcelain tile with half an image on it? A faded photograph? A picture would be better, it wouldn't be as weathered as jade. After they'd finished ransacking Dr. Shi's house, her floor was covered in photographs. She'd been so pretty when she was young, they no longer looked like her. People had stepped all over those photos, but her face still beamed through each footprint, a smile that had been trodden on.

Our ragged breathing filled the night with urgency and yearning. We'd never imagined or even dreamed of what we were going to see. I'd never thought I'd encounter a genuine princess in this lifetime. Princesses hadn't existed for such a long time, and even if they did, we'd have to call them Comrade So-And-So. A dead princess, beautiful as pale jade, mesmerizing. She'd died with her title intact, and to call her "Lady Comrade" now would be unsuitable, she couldn't acknowledge it, wouldn't answer to that name, so she was even more a real princess than a living princess would have been. I was going to see a real princess. We all were.

*

When we reached the spot, an enormous excavator truck was digging into the earth by electric light beneath the winter sky. Nothing more. Despite its name, this place had nothing to offer us, no shattered fragments and no princess. Beneath our feet was newly churned mud. Nothing to disguise this place, an ordinary construction site. The truck bit into the ground again and again. Nobody was watching except for us, not that there was much to look at—an excavator truck is nothing special, just a piece of machinery, and we were there to see a person, albeit a dead one, but that's still more meaningful than a piece of machinery, mechanical things are worth even less than corpses—they've never been alive. Which bastard did this, making us watch a machine rather than a princess? Why had we come all this way to see a crappy old truck? Pure disappointment filled us in an instant. We grabbed clods of dirt and flung them at the excavator, but it didn't notice and kept working. It couldn't even feel pain. Can something free of pain understand when other people are sad? Can it? Fang Yong's hand dangled by his side. He was clutching a broken plank but didn't throw it. We turned around and went home. On the way back, I looked down and sniffed but couldn't smell my own sweat. We'd lost our passion. If I walked backward, I could think back to when we were imagining the princess—those images were now entangled with the road-side trees and wooden fences. Facing ahead, there was only the excavator truck. We walked along, seven kids. Fang Yong spoke first: We climbed up the highest mound of earth and saw the princess's burial pit, someone had lit a ring of candles around her, throwing a pinkish glow onto her skin, as if she were still alive. There was no one there at all, the workmen were on their dinner break, it was just the seven of us and her. We knelt to look at the princess. All but seven stars in the sky were hidden, and there was no moon, so the seven of us stood in the positions indicated by the stars. The princess opened her mouth and words came out. She told us to bring her away, to conceal her with our eyes. Look at me, she said, don't blink or move until I tell you to shut your eyes, and I'll be hidden in your seven pairs of eyes, so when you open them again there'll be nothing here but this ring of candles. We did as she instructed and sure enough, she was gone when we opened our eyes. The candles still glittered in a circle. She's snuck into our eyes, a portion each for the seven of us and all of her in our hearts.

We continued to retreat, listening to Fang Yong's story, growing entranced and entering into it, adding details and filling in missing elements. Later, someone suggested the princess should come back to life. Whenever the seven of us were together, she'd appear to sing for us and do our laundry. I later realized we'd braided our own lives with the story of *Snow White*, because we'd been to visit a princess and there happened to be seven of us. Now our existences were tightly bound to a fairy tale.

Reluctant to go home, we huddled against the wall and continued the story. Stars twinkled in the sky above us, and our quiet fantasies brought warmth to the winter night.

The broken plank Fang Yong lugged back later became the evidence we'd wave at the grown-ups we told our fairy tale to. After much retelling and expanding, the story of the Princess's Tomb grew much more vivid. When it came back round to us, we listened with eyes wide and mouths open. Some people said the candles had grown out of the earth, others said seven demons appeared and dismembered the princess, so the construction site that night was filled with the sounds of chewing and crunching bones. Also, the baubles decorating her body were steeped in poison, and anyone who dared put them on would die instantly. Still others claimed the princess's beauty was a trap, and when some pervert flung himself on her late at night, his *down there* rotted in an instant. This last story even mentioned his name, someone we knew: the coal delivery man. Probably whoever came up with that assigned him this role because his body was black with coal dust, and therefore he must loathe the pale jade-like beauty of the princess.

We'd never expected that some people, in creating fairy tales, would turn their minds to eating flesh and crunching bones. Humanity was all fetid bowels, and the collective of grown-ups even more so.

Lots more people went to see the uncovered tomb, walking there when the buses got too crowded. For a few days, the west end of Chang'an Road was full of the crowds viewing the princess's corpse, who'd come away with a story about her. The weirdest thing was none of us heard the words "excavator truck" from a single person's lips. We began to think we hadn't actually gone to the construction site that night, that the story we made up later was the truth.

Big Qi came to find us again. He'd been there that afternoon but found no one there, only a big poster with the slogan "Don't be a worshipful descendant of the old feudal order" pasted to the arm of an excavator truck. Finally, we all heard it: someone saying the words "excavator truck."

URN PEOPLE

As a child, I enjoyed wandering the streets and browsing three types of shops: wireless stores, bookstores, and pawn shops. I walked everywhere, clutching a few coins in my hand, never quite enough for a bus ride. Like now, elementary schools back then had no classes on Saturday afternoons, and I could always find a gang of friends to hang out with. We'd walk from the Military Museum to Xidan, about ten li or an hour's walk. As we strolled along, we reminded each other not to let strangers touch our heads. The grown-ups were always warning us that the streets were full of tricksters who specialized in kidnapping children. How it worked was they'd smear a hallucinogen on their hand and pat your head. After the drug took effect, you'd see nothing but endless water and waves around you, apart from a trail of solid ground behind the guy, and so you'd have to no choice but to follow him. Children taken in this way were sold to gangs for street performances. They'd cut off your tongue and stick you in an urn barely large enough to hold you, with only your head sticking out. Every day they'd feed you a little until your body was a deformed mass and your head swelled up. Then they'd take you out and exhibit you by the side of the road. These unfortunates were known as urn people.

When I heard these stories as a kid, I believed I'd be kidnapped someday by a trickster, winding up as an urn person fit only to be humiliated all day long. Then one day I'd spot my family in the audience watching me, and they'd recognize me too. After an emotional reunion, I'd be rescued from my misery.

This kept not happening. We paid attention to grown-ups in the street, but they largely ignored us. If someone looked dodgy we gave them a wide berth, our minds filled with imagined terrors. We always got back home safely.

All the way from second to sixth grade, I often wandered up and down the street, sometimes bringing home a pair of headphones, sometimes a book. The pawn shops were always full of these things: cumbersome clocks, hookahs ornamented with pictures, violins missing their strings, wooden radio sets with wire mesh speakers, pocket watches, old leather jackets smelling of camphor, water hookahs, old carpets. These places had an abundance of merchandise, each aged item with its own promise of an unusual history, stranded there in distress like an urn person.

Occasionally someone came in with an object they wanted to sell. The man behind the counter would examine the splayed-open watch with a loupe before pronouncing, "You can sell it for so-many yuan, or pawn it for so-many yuan." If the customer wasn't anxious, he'd leave it there as security, otherwise he'd say, "Sell it, then!" There are always people on this earth desperate for ready cash. They'd put down the watch, count their money, and depart hurriedly.

According to hearsay, there were Beijingers who made a living flipping pawned goods. They'd see something priced a little low, buy it, and sell it elsewhere. You could make eight or ten yuan that way. Of course, you needed a good eye and experience to pull this off.

The pawn shops were piled high with items, while I was preparing to be sent down. All the officials in Beijing were hastily joining cadre schools or Third Front industrial bases, and everything salable they possessed was hauled off to hock. Added to this, the Red Guards were constantly ransacking houses, and pawnbrokers received much of the resultant debris. Sofas and pianos took up the most space. I saw a grand piano going for a hundred and eighty yuan. Another time, an old man turned up with a leather sofa on a flatbed truck and the shop-owner only offered five yuan for it. The guy said that wouldn't even cover the truck hire, but in the end he agreed.

My dad was leaving too, and our house was full of cardboard boxes and straw rope. Before his departure, he asked me to deal with a stack of foreign-language books, weighty hardcover editions. I lugged them to a second-hand bookstore in Xidan on my bicycle. Ahead of me in the line were a woman and her daughter, who was about my age. So many books. The counter clerk flipped through them, saying which he wanted and which he didn't. Many were in sets—I remember one, *The Extensive Records of the Taiping Era*, being bought for five cents per volume. The girl stood to one side looking embarrassed, as if she were doing something shameful. The clerk told the mother he'd take the rejected books for the price of scrap paper. She thought about it and said no, tying them up instead and asking me to help her carry them out. As I loaded them onto her bicycle, she casually handed one to me. The girl met my eye as she left, looking a little more relaxed—she'd realized I was also there to sell books. The woman's gift was *Twenty Thousand Leagues Under the Sea*, a book we weren't supposed to read back then.

When it was my turn, the clerk glanced at my pile of foreign-language books and refused to take any of them, unless it was as scrap paper. My father had said, as I was heading out, be sure to sell them, no matter how little they offer. But perhaps he hadn't considered they would be turned into scrap? Still, I said, "Deal!" The clerk picked up the first book and ripped off its cloth-bound cover. "Why did you do that?" I asked. He replied, "They're too heavy, we can't include their weight." Volume by volume, he tore the covers off and tossed their naked remains onto the scales. I picked the hardcovers off the floor (two bundles of books fetched only one yuan twenty-five). They were no use to me, but I felt they should be laid to rest somewhere more suitable, not left by the buying counter to be trampled by countless feet.

My dad reacted very calmly when I told him how little I'd been paid, as if that was all the books had ever been worth. He told me to keep the money and accepted the stack of discarded covers, like a man receiving his child back after it had been turned into an urn person.

Sometime after that, I used the money to buy two items from a pawn shop. One was a desk lamp with a carved mahogany base in the shape of a dragon, a hand-painted silk shade like a six-sided pagoda with dangling tassels and a porcelain snuff-dish on its base. I paid a yuan for that because I liked the dragon. My other purchase was a little wooden cabinet with tiny, fully functional drawers, brass handles and corner brackets. That set me back sixty cents.

After a few years, both objects vanished. Perhaps they were lost during a move after I was sent down, or perhaps they're still in some remote corner of my parents' house. I've never gone back to look for them.

THE LITTLE RASCALS

1.

My family moved to Yangfangdian in 1960. All around our building were vegetable fields, and in the midst of this greenery were white stone tablets (commonly known as "turtleback stones") on which were inscribed huge characters, most of which we couldn't recognize as we stared up at them. It didn't help that there wasn't any punctuation at all. Nonetheless, we persisted in reading them out to demonstrate the joy of learning. Several children would stand in a group and chant in unison: Something something built something something stone something something something memorial. Some lines had not a single comprehensible word, and still we'd something-something-something-something our way through, no shortcuts. I get nostalgic now thinking of a gaggle of kids chorusing "something."

(The other day, a child on the bus I was on began reading signs out loud: Something something snack bar, something something store, something-something-something-something. Then he read "public toilet" as "public to let," leaving the passengers in stitches.)

I was in sixth grade when the Cultural Revolution began. The stone tablets were knocked over and left lying flat on the ground, so you could feel as well as read the words. Tracing the strokes of each character, you imagined writing fine calligraphy. The falling strokes brought a sensation of freedom, while the vertical ones made us careful. Regretfully, we couldn't bring these words home. They had sprouted from the stone and couldn't easily be taken away.

The boy nicknamed "Cop" told us there was a way to capture them: place a sheet of paper over the words and shade with a pencil until the character appeared. In the days after that we frantically tried to copy every word, and many other kids joined in. Getting these imprints really felt like a feat of artistry, and the characters we gathered were exactly like the ones on the stone.

Our project ended the day someone smashed the words with a hammer. They lay on the ground into pieces, some still vaguely recognizable, others so shattered even the strokes were impossible to make out, and the only way to read them was to go: something-something-something, something-something-something.

2.

The itinerant barbers who wandered the streets carried a noisemaker called a "summoner." After reading *Mr. Jin Shoushen's Life in Old Beijing*, I learned how dignified and powerful these instruments were during the Qing Dynasty. Like the tuning fork I encountered later on, the sound they made set my teeth on edge.

Unlike knife-sharpeners today shaking their strings of metal plates, the ones back then blew a small brass horn. Just two notes, a fifth apart, sounding like "baah-ba"—slang for "shit."

When the knife-sharpener arrived at our courtyard, all the children cheered up. The pleasure of watching him at work grinding blades and scissors was secondary, though. Our main joy was when he raised his horn, an instant before he could blow, all the children would jog a short way off and shout in unison, "What do you eat?" And his horn would go, "Baah-ba," as if it were answering, "Shit." They timed it perfectly. After this exchange, they'd run off clapping one another on the shoulder in victory at successfully playing an enormous trick on the man. When he got annoyed and went after them, they grew even merrier, dashing in all directions, waiting at a distance for him to blow again. The poor peddler kept wanting to sound his horn again and having to stop himself.

One knife-sharpener, after suffering in this way a few times, arrived at our courtyard pretending he was about to sound his horn, but when the kids called their usual taunt, he didn't follow through. After a few attempts, the children gave up. Then he cried out, "What am I to you?" Then he blew "Baah-ba," like "Papa," like he was our daddy. No one laughed—the kids had lost and would never play this game again. This man's business suffered, though—the other grown-ups felt he'd taken the joke too far.

3.

In the summer, the many pipes in our cellar leaked yellowish liquid that spattered all over the floor. Apart from these pipes, the space held picks, shovels, and a pile of straw sacks, beneath which were woodlice. They ran away so slowly it was easy to tread on them.

A family of feral cats lived down there too. They were ferocious and prowled boldly during the day. We felt uneasy at the sight of them, itching all over as if our bodies were sprouting fur.

One kid went down there all the time and knew where the light switches were. When he flicked them there'd be an echo—*pah! pah!*—and the dark areas would grow bright, leaving our faces no longer familiar, shadowy beneath the lamps.

Once we came upon a whole stack of paper sleeves, smaller than an envelope but larger than a playing card. We were delighted, using them first as gambling counters for our game of throwing apricot stones, then finding a pencil to scribble swear words on them, which we'd pass to each other. Someone who got called a "bastard" wrote some lines on another card, although looking at them now I hesitate to call this a poem.

You can curse me, I won't cry. Your momma is a Yankee spy.
Spies all have pointy snouts, so your mom's a hairy cow.
Hairy cows have four legs, so your mom has teeth like pegs.
Peg-teeth can't stay shut, so your mom's a big old slut.
Slut's a good word for her mate, so your mom's a shriveled date . . .

(This was probably my first encounter with this kind of linked rhyme.)

After we got bored of cursing and being cursed, someone blew into a paper bag till it was puffed up, twisted the mouth shut, and stomped on it so it went *bang*. We got worked up and all gave it a go, until the whole place was full of explosions, shaking up the dust.

Each little paper sack was stamped with the words "Oral use." We didn't know what that meant, but presumably these were from a pharmacy, indicating medicine to be taken by mouth. To increase the magnificence of the occasion, we took to shouting "Oral use," before stamping to deflate the bag, leaving our feet slightly numb.

Oral use—*bang!* Oral use—*bang!* Excited by this crisp slogan and thunderous response, we vied to one-up each other. Some guys didn't crimp their paper sacks tightly enough, and those went "Oral use— *pfft.*" This was known as a drooping turd, and whoever produced one received the contempt of the room.

Oral use—*bang!* The sound must have carried to the outside, and soon the yard was full of flying scraps of paper. *Bang!* The explosions kept sounding. The grown-ups anxiously stuck their heads out their windows and stared foolishly, uncertain what was going on, baffled by our cries of "Oral use."

4.

Our route home from school took us past a construction site. A laborer was using a sharpened bamboo pole to prepare "hemp blades" (that is, crushed hemp fibers). The shredded plant matter was gathered in a pile, ready to be mixed with lime and used as a sealant. Another guy was bending metal wires, just the right thickness to be used as a slingshot.

Past that was a vegetable farm. A dog stood in the field, looking ferocious. We knew how to bend down and fling stones, but our technique was far from perfect, and when the dog came running toward us we fled.

We saw a locust tree covered in "hanging devils," which felt cool and ticklish crawling along our palms. Like silkworms, they fed on leaves and had devoured so much of the crown that from a distance, it resembled a broken fishing net. This kind of tree also housed many sparrows, who picked away at the buffet of hanging devils.

Sometimes we pooled our money to buy a popsicle. When we peeled off the wrapper, the sun made it emit vapor-like steam. The first person to have it bit off a chunk and spat it into his hands to suck at. If he went too fast, he'd cry out, Brainfreeze!

We hung out on a cement terrace, nice and smooth, perfect for playing picture cards. One little boy liked using a slate pencil to draw airplanes and battleships there, making warlike noises as he sketched. A high-pitched sound indicated speed, while each explosion had reverberations of decreasing volume. After covering his territory with the apparatus of war, he'd add in a single figure wearing a court official's hat and epaulets, labeling it "Commander" followed by his name. Getting his commands mixed up, he'd cry "Halt!" instead of "Attention!" and then "Reporting!" He depicted himself rather dashingly and refused to play with us. We'd shout in unison, "Commander, sir, permission to report! Your wife is in Taipei / her pants have gone away / her panties have a tear / to show off her rear." Then we'd produce our own slate pens and draw dozens of bombs, making our own noises as we scribbled all over his warscape. Beneath his name we'd add "is my son."

He ambushed me and another boy from behind a mound of dirt. We flung pebbles at each other, screaming "Charge!" and "Duck!" I scored a direct hit to his head, and blood poured over his ear. The other boy and I ran over to him, terrified. His hand was pressed to his face, blood seeping between his fingers, but he didn't cry. I definitely threw the stone that hit him. Looking around, I saw a dirty playing card on the ground and picked it up to staunch his wound. The King of Hearts' sword was quickly smeared with blood. I suddenly didn't know what to do, and tears dribbled down my face.

That summer, I returned home one day exhausted from playing. Opening the door, I was startled to see him sitting at our family table eating grapes. I thought I must have gone to the wrong house and looked again, but there was no mistake. I asked how he got in, and he said his balcony door key also opened our front door. I tried for myself and sure enough, it did.

Looking back, seeing him sitting there calmly popping a grape into his mouth made it feel like he was family.

5.

There was a pair of twins no one could tell apart. They always dressed identically, and their voices sounded the same too. When no one else was around, they had each other as playmates for marbles, kick-attack, or flipping cigarette packets folded into triangles. It must have looked like someone playing against himself. They'd fight too, shoving at each other, like a guy grabbing his own shirt collar, shouting at himself. Or perhaps someone split in two, both halves at war with each other. However you looked at it, they were a real-life illusion—there was no way to believe they were a single person, but it was also hard to see them as separate individuals. For a time, many local kids argued over this puzzle.

We had a game called "powder bag": with a pin, you pricked the shape of a turtle into a sheet of thick card, which you then folded into an envelope and filled with quicklime. With this hidden in your palm, you went up to another kid and patted him warmly on the back, a friendly gesture. The turtle print showed up especially clearly on dark blue clothes. Ideally your victim wouldn't realize what you'd done, so everyone could laugh behind his back. If he walked into class or went home without brushing off the mark, the prankster was considered to have won.

Powder-bagging the twins wasn't easy. They were like a single person with two pairs of eyes, watching his own back.

It wasn't easy to get them undetected, and even if you did, the other one would quickly notice and brush off his brother's shirt. This made the game much less entertaining, and after a while we stopped trying. Their backs remained free of grayish marks—clean, but also very lonely, even desolate.

One day, having nothing to do, I lay sprawled by the window looking out and happened to see the twins each holding a powder bag, sneakily marking each other as they played marbles. Both boys' backs were covered in turtle marks, and each seemed thrilled, unaware his brother was doing the same thing. I detected a species of amusement that arose from destructiveness. They still appeared like someone unable to get on with himself, but no longer the same person. That day, I learned to tell them apart.

6.

Castor beans are shiny as little eyeballs, their hard shells encasing an oily blob. Plant one and by fall, the resulting castor plant would tower over us, its hollow green stem ready to be snapped into lengths that made vicious ammunition for slingshots. The castor oil fruit came wrapped in a spiky skin that split open when dry—you'd see them all over the ground.

Castor beans aren't edible, but if you collected enough you could take them to the provision shop to exchange for redbean pastries, which were delicious and, like all flaky baked goods, left a sheen of oil on the fingers after eating.

That spring, we collected more than twenty castor beans, which we planted in a vacant lot near where we lived. An open ditch ran nearby, and we used its black soil for fertilizer, loosening the ground first with a metal sheet.

Three days later, we dug up the seeds to see how they were doing, partly because we were afraid they'd gone missing, partly to see if they'd sprouted yet. They seemed fine—there was only one we couldn't account for. We also moved away two anthills, afraid the insects would steal our seedlings.

When the first green shoots appeared, they'd sway gently in the breeze. There were only a dozen or so, too tender to bring home. We worried excessively about them, and that summer a few of us behaved like the worst kinds of parents.

We'd go to that bit of ground every single day, making sure to pee while we were there, because we'd heard this would add nutrients to the soil. We worked hard at this, sometimes even saving our morning urine and carrying it to the site. After a while, the area acquired a familiar stench of piss. We were sure that the stronger that odor, the better our seedlings would grow.

Sure enough, they shot upward vigorously and by summer vacation were almost as tall as us, their branches strong and thick, their leaves the size of a human face. They didn't need much protection from us now, and passersby sometimes got cut by the sharp leaves if they weren't careful. They were so strong we felt superfluous—these plants seemed mightier than us, more mature and independent. We had to raise our heads to see them in their entirety. A disheartening thought—the castor plants had outgrown our hearts and become strangers to us.

We stopped going there every day. A bladderful of urine at the feet of a great castor plant felt like a pathetic offering. They stood, proud and green, against sun and wind and rain.

After school started again, the castor plants grew yellower day after day, and their seed pods appeared at the tip of each branch, waiting to be gathered, like high school students ready to make their mark on the world. Not one of us went to collect them. This was the fall of 1966, and most of our classmates were busy ransacking people's houses, putting up big-character posters, forming themselves into units, linking up with other students across the country, marching in the streets—and the castor seeds no longer mattered.

.

PART TWO:
GRAINS OF SAND IN THE WIND

A MUG

I've had an enamel mug for twenty-two years now, and never once used it. The last time I moved house, it tumbled from the depths of a crate, still looking brand new, emblazoned with the bright red slogan "Up to the mountains, down to the countryside, for glory," next to a scarlet flower over green terraced fields.

Gazing at the cup, a cacophony of energetic drumbeats came back to me, along with red posters, straw ropes, wooden crates, newly-issued military-green padded cotton jackets, tears of excitement or sorrow, letters written in blood, the gleam of a lamp as my mother stitched a mattress late into the night . . .

August 16, 1969, Beijing Train Station. My father emerged from behind a pillar, wearing his "reactionary authority" hat. He'd been granted leave from detention in the cowshed to see me off. Behind his glasses, his eyes didn't contain too much sorrow. Handing me a violin, he said I could amuse myself with music if there was any spare time during my "re-education through poverty" in the farming village. I accepted it, not knowing what to say. All this time, I'd been longing to get away from Beijing, my home, and the housing estate that despised me.

My father left before the train did—they'd only let him out for a short while. Perhaps he couldn't bear to hear the bell as the train departed. I gave up the window seat to some schoolmates. Then the bell went off, and gales of sobbing suddenly erupted both on and off the train. I'd never again witness so many people crying at the same time, like a river flooding its banks. My eyes remained dry and I sat upright, thinking there was nothing to cry about. I imagined the Great Northern Waste as a place where I'd be able to breathe freely.

This was my first train ride, and I watched excitedly as the endlessly changing landscape flickered past. My schoolmates stayed up all night, chatting away, horsing around. I can no longer remember what we talked about, a gaggle of sixteen-year-old overgrown children. We treated the journey as if it were no more than a short excursion.

The Great Northern Waste is accurately named. Sky above, ground below, the individual caught between them. Here your breath grew weak. All that seemed solid were the ground, the clouds, the heavens—the natural world, with humanity as an afterthought.

On October 1, 1969, it began to snow in Dedu County, where the Heilongjiang Production and Construction Corps First Division Sixth Regiment was stationed. This came upon us quickly, before we'd even had time to unpack our winter clothes. Without stoves, and not knowing how to make a fire, the young people of Class Three-Three slumped on the icy platform in a half-built assembly hall, listening to the National Day Celebrations from Tiananmen. The familiar sounds were muffled by the falling snow, distanced by distorted noises from the semiconductor. There were more than twenty of us guys, gloomy from the cold and homesickness. No one said a word. We didn't know what to say.

I got out my violin and played one of the three or four simple tunes I knew: the Russian folk song "The Vast Plains," a melancholy tune about the impending death of a carriage driver. The music merged with the falling snow to form a desolate scene. When I put down my instrument, I saw that almost everyone was weeping—some had their arms over their faces to hide it, others stared straight at me with wet eyes, not speaking. I put it back into its case, and in an instant my tears were flowing too, plopping hollowly onto the violin.

This was the only time we cried together; the incident was never repeated. There are times when tears can be more powerful than fire, and emotions tempered in their blaze will be hard as steel.

A TUBE OF TOOTHPASTE

By 1971, I'd been in the Great Northern Waste a year and a half. Most people had visited home by then (not officially—they snuck out). Because my father's case hadn't been settled, I resisted the urge myself. He wrote in April to say he'd been released from the cowshed and the matter was being cleared up. He hoped I'd be able to visit. I applied for leave a few times but was denied. Finally, a friend and I decided to run away together.

It was now May, and the snow was starting to melt. One morning, we slipped away from the muddy ground of the reservoir work site and sprinted to the train station. In order to dodge the ticket inspector, we waited for the train to start moving before jumping on board.

It wasn't that we couldn't afford tickets—we had thirty yuan between us—but we wanted to hang on to that money and spend it in Beijing. Educated youths mostly didn't buy train tickets on these clandestine trips home. It was a journey of two days and a night, and we saw it as an opportunity to hone our skills. (It looks implausible now that I write it down, but this really did happen.)

The money needed to be well-concealed; if we were caught and searched by the guard, they'd confiscate any cash they found. Just before we left, I'd squeezed half the toothpaste from a tube, ripped the other end open, inserted the folded banknotes, and rolled it up again.

We reached Harbin without incident and changed trains, then a guard kicked us off at Shuangcheng. It was midnight, and icy rain was falling. The filthy, cold waiting room was empty apart from a bearded man with a scarred face who kept circling us menacingly, until we decided to stand outside. It was pitch dark here, not even a scrap of light. Quite a while went by before I discovered we were in a field full of cattle by almost smashing my face into a cow's rump. The cattle stood quietly in the rain, unnerving us so much we retreated to the waiting room. The bearded man came over and told us, "Don't bother paying your fares, you can sneak onto the next one." We ignored him, bought short-distance tickets, and boarded the next train at dawn.

Dodging inspectors all the way, we finally arrived in Tianjin. It took us more than an hour to find a way out of the station without using the ticket gates. In the end, we jumped through a bathroom window.

We were almost at Beijing now, exhausted and grubby, but also exhilarated. After half a day's leisurely exploration of Tianjin city, we found it impossible to get back into the station. They weren't selling platform tickets.

I can no longer remember whether it was my friend or I who refused to spend any more money on travel, but in any case we didn't touch the cash in my toothpaste tube.

The next morning saw two young people walking along the road from Tianjin to Beijing (don't laugh at this foolishness—foolish ideas were everywhere at the time). We tried to thumb a ride, but no one would stop for us. We walked through a light drizzle till nightfall, when we passed Yangchun. Dead tired by this point, we swayed along like a pair of shadows. Finally, my friend leaned against a tree trunk and said he wanted a little nap, and I slumped next to him.

I don't know how much time passed. Then someone was shaking us awake.

"Hey! Wake up, wake up. Where are you going? Why are you sleeping in the rain?"

It was a truck driver. His vehicle was parked a short distance away.

"Back to Beijing. We're too tired to go further, and don't have the money for a ride."

"Where have you come from?"

"The Great Northern Waste."

"Which division? Are you from the '69 batch?"

"Yes, we went in '69. First Division."

"Ah! My boy is in First Division too. What do you think you're doing walking home? Get in, quick. I'll give you a ride."

Dripping wet, we scrambled into the back of the truck, but he said it would be too cold back there, come sit in the cab.

We'd finally met a good person. He kept asking us how things were in the Great Northern Waste and said seeing us made us think of his son. He worried that his son would try to sneak home like us.

Before long, we'd passed Tongtan and reached the North Kiln. The man stopped the truck and said he wasn't going any farther, but gave us a yuan to get a ride home. We refused but he kept insisting until we accepted the money, trying to look as if we really were penniless. We got a taxi the rest of the way. Afterward, I felt uneasy at having cheated a good person.

It left a bad taste in my mouth. Although we spent the rest of the money, we made sure to leave one yuan untouched in the toothpaste tube, hoping to return it to him if our paths crossed again.

A BASIN

I'm not sure when it started, but we've begun to be surrounded by plastic. Plastic floor coverings, plastic wallpaper, plastic washbasins, plastic chopping boards, plastic bags, plastic false teeth. It's everywhere, though hopefully we'll never reach the point of plastic dumplings or hamburgers. Plastic is a substance with no sense of history. Like an overnight millionaire, it creates a sense of resentment and helplessness.

So many plastic objects have crammed their way into my life, but I've steadfastly refused to wash my face in a plastic basin. Instead, I use the most common enamel variety; bits of coating flake off when I'm not paying attention, revealing the rust-covered past.

The first winter after we arrived in the Great Northern Waste, the boys of Three-Three moved from the freezing cold stage into an already-crowded dorm. Not that the place could be called small—there were at least sixteen people in each room of double-decker bunks—but it was tiny compared to the gigantic ones nearby that housed eighty people each.

In a small place like this, morning ablutions became a problem. Only three or four people at a time could squat down to wash up, and there were frequent collisions of one person's head with another's ass. The dorm provided a large rack on which hung our basins, sixteen of them in stacks of two or three. During one spot check, a local man named Old Li sneered, "Why do you youngsters need so many basins? One should be enough." Who could have predicted we'd soon have to put his words into practice?

Where we stayed, the well house was next to a distillery with a thatched hut where they stored raw materials. One night, this hut burst into flames.

Putting out the fire made us feel full of responsibility and vigor. Each of us grabbed a basin and dashed outside. The well handle cranked nonstop as basin after basin of water was passed back into the building. When we ran out of water, we started filling them with snow. The basins flew back and forth, we flung them up and they came back down. Those on the building bravely stood near the fire, throwing water, urging us on, shouting encouragement. Our clothes got soaked, and a short while later began freezing over. We ran to and fro in armor of ice. Such excitement, selflessness and unity, filling us with strength. Fortunately there were many of us, hence many basins, and the fire shrank. When it was almost extinguished, a schoolmate who'd been one of the first to clamber onto the roof slipped and fell, scorching his hand on a smoldering piece of wood.

When the fire was out, we returned to the dorm covered in soot, still full of excitement and tension from our efforts. Only when we wanted to wash our faces did we realize we'd left our basins outside. There was only one left on the rack, belonging to the guy with the burned hand. He'd been the first to rush out and hadn't thought to grab his basin.

The next morning, people from the various dorms headed out to the burnt-out site to retrieve their property. I'd never seen so many broken basins in my life. All night long they'd been thrown, dropped, stepped on. They looked deformed, dented or full of holes. We later heard that the ones in better condition had been snatched up by the girls, who'd arrived earlier. Our group didn't manage to salvage a single basin.

Old Li said, "It was just an old thatched hut, you should have let it burn. It wasn't even worth what a couple of basins cost. Now look, the ground's covered in broken basins, and you got someone injured."

These were dispiriting words, but we didn't agree. The previous night had demonstrated a certain spirit—what did a basin matter, compared with that spirit? Not one of us was upset at the loss of his basin. Afterward, Old Li was censured for saying such strange things.

The guy with the burned hand later reflected on his selfishness while self-criticizing. He said he too had a selfish heart, not grabbing his own basin when they ran out to fight the fire, leaving him with the only unbroken one in the whole building. I felt doubtful about this for a long time afterward, not sure whether he really felt this way, or if he'd said these words for effect, because they were stirring and deep. I knew it was pure chance that his basin was the only one left, because that night had been absolute chaos, and we'd grabbed basins at random, not necessarily our own.

Afterward, there were many things I could no longer look at so innocently. Unexpected words appeared out of nowhere, shattering the passion and certainty of my sixteen-year-old self. I even started thinking that Old Li hadn't been wrong, especially after someone from another company burned their face trying to save a pile of firewood.

Youth is a concept whose meaning isn't easy to grasp. You might as well try to wrap your mind around every era, every event. The word doesn't really evoke any special memories for me. Perhaps I'll have to wait till the age when every other sentence begins with "back then" before I truly understand it.

BLISTER BEETLE

Time to take your temperature. The horsefaced nurse walked over and stuck her thermometer beneath his armpit. A smile flashed across his face, a vacant grin. Horseface came back and sat directly opposite him, glaring at the thermometer clamped beneath his arm, eyes like a machine gun. A minute passed, and he hadn't had the opportunity to stick his hand down his collar to shake the glass tube.

*

There were many ways to make the mercury rise. The most common was for your armpit to actually reach 38 degrees Celsius, which counted as a fever. If your body couldn't generate this heat on its own, you'd have to rely on physics. Of all the available methods, he chose the least obtrusive—shaking the tip of the thermometer so the mercury gently flowed toward it. Ten swift jerks would nudge it into the desirable zone of 38.5 to 39 degrees. Of course, you had to be careful not to use too much strength. He'd practiced countless times and after destroying six thermometers, managed to master the technique.

This was his seventh time in this chair having his temperature taken. Horseface sat opposite him, so stationary that she could have been a propaganda poster. He beamed ingratiatingly, but her stare went directly to his bad tooth. After that, whenever he was tempted to smile again, he kept his mouth firmly shut.

No two people used the same method of simulating fever. Lion Snout clamped the thermometer under his left armpit, tugging it back and forth with his right hand so friction could heat it up. He tried it once with a stolen instrument, but his movements were too big, too obvious, and the mercury took ages to rise. By the time it reached 38 degrees, his whole underarm area was red and smelt of rotten eggs. Old Jian from the cafeteria snuck in a bun straight from the steamer and plunged the thermometer into its scalding center while the nurse was distracted. Unfortunately he misjudged the timing—by the time the nurse came back, it had climbed to 42 degrees and he was sent straight to the emergency room. Five minutes later, he was out again. Diagnosis: the bun had cooled down.

As for the trick our guy invented, it came to him while having a smoke. You make a flaccid cigarette firm again by tamping it so the tobacco gravitates to one end. Nothing can resist inertia, including the thermometer's mercury. He didn't share his innovation with a single soul.

Two minutes passed. Growing bored, Horseface opened a drawer to search for something or other. His right hand gingerly went up, stroked his hair, then casually slid inside his collar. His movements were natural and smooth, like someone scratching an old itch. He kept one eye on her whitecapped mane, hoping the drawer's contents were interesting enough to keep her head down—a love letter, a photograph of herself, something. One, three, six shakes. Horseface pushed the drawer back in. Still only 37.5 degrees. At the last possible second, he gave it a vigorous bounce and heard a crisp sound from his armpit, a snap that pierced right into his guts. It had broken. Something warm and wet slid down his ribs, and the left side of his torso felt stiff and icy cold. Horseface looked up, the large whites of her eyes shrouding him.

"Hand it over."

"Hand what over?" He turned his head as if to look at the door behind him.

"The thermometer!"

He felt around as if his hand had only slipped inside his collar by mistake. Finally, he fished out the beheaded implement. Horseface's face grew even longer. She brought the glass tube over to a ray of sunshine to examine it, then scribbled something on a piece of paper, ripped it from her pad and handed it to him.

"Go and pay! No fever today."

He stood and took the note respectfully. The warm slime glooped onto the floor, and he saw it quivering brightly there, breaking into separate globules. He turned and walked out of the stable. Outside, he saw that the paper read, "One thermometer—2.65 yuan."

The girl at the counter miraculously revealed a secret. "What's wrong with this batch of educated youths? Doing medical discharges—you lot ruined 30 thermometers in five days."

The cashier's words were right, medical discharges were something you did. You did this or that until you could produce something wrong with you so they'd send you back home, back to Shanghai or Beijing or wherever. Our guy was also the one who did Blossom's medical discharge. (Isn't "did" a nasty-sounding word? Like doing your girlfriend or some other woman, fooling around; but then we talk about doing revolution or reproduction, it's doing my head in.) The day of Blossom's ECG, he brought along a bottle of grain spirits and some tea leaves. Just beforehand, he got her to gulp down six mouthfuls of spirits, then run up and down the stairs to the fifth floor four times. Finally, she had to chew two bunches of tea leaves to get rid of the alcohol smell. This produced an irregular heartbeat of 138, a diagnosis of heart disease, and a ticket back to Shanghai. The night before her departure, Blossom kept kissing him, then crying, then kissing him again, tears and saliva mingling on his face. His own heartbeat shot up to 143. Her embrace was more effective than grain spirits.

No fever today no fever today no fever today. He walked back to the dormitory, which stood empty—everyone was at work. He sat for a while before pulling out the jar, which gleamed in the sunlight. There were five bugs inside, dead blister beetles, dark velvety fuzz over their backs, a large yellow spot on each front wing, like two eyes staring out of a black face. How sleek these creatures looked, even as corpses. Black and yellow. He had a fuzzy memory that only emperors in movies used these colors these together. Or had he remembered wrongly? Perhaps they were funeral colors. What if eating these things were to kill him? He screwed the lid back on and stowed the jar back beneath his blanket.

His last visit home to Shanghai, he bought a pack of "sponge head" (that is, filter-tip) cigarettes and went to find Grandpa Li, the trash collector. Grandpa Li used to have a stall in the alleyway, selling herbal remedies that cured some patients and killed others. Then someone revealed that his pills were composed of sawdust, brick powder, honey and athlete's foot cream. At a struggle session, Grandpa Li memorized the Quotations of Chairman Mao to defend himself with. "Life can be heavier than Mount Tai, or lighter than a goose feather." The grannies who'd denounced him gave him a good beating, and afterward he changed jobs and became a trash collector. That day, after a couple of cigarettes, our guy asked Grandpa Li what could produce blood in the urine. He'd asked the same thing of Third Uncle, who worked at the hospital, and got the answer, "Kidney inflammation ought to do it." Useless. Of course it would be very nice to get kidney inflammation, but that couldn't be arranged. He tried again, asking if there was anything he could do in the absence of illness? Third Uncle looked startled. He might be able to cure illnesses, but causing them was outside the scope of his job. That day, Grandpa Li lit his third cigarette, then motioned for him to bring his ear closer, into which he whispered two words that sent a chill through his eardrum.

"Blister beetle."

He asked more questions, but Grandpa just smoked, not speaking. It wasn't till he was about to leave that the old man instructed him, "Only eat half of one at a time."

These bugs lived in the fields to the south. He caught five and dried them, then poured them into the jar like precious gems and brought them back with him.

The night of the broken thermometer, when the rest of the dorm was asleep, he reached beneath his blanket and pulled out the jar, stroking one of the little creatures. Its fur gleamed like satin, and the two yellow points glared fiercely at him. He broke it between his fingers and ate the half with the head attached. Lying down again, he felt the half-insect scurrying back and forth in his stomach. He clamped his mouth tightly shut, afraid it might crawl out.

He dreamed he was pissing inside a temple, with all the Buddhas watching him. A stream of red sprayed out of him, dribbled off the walls, and became the sunrise. Blossom called to him from within the light, still teary-eyed. In the middle of the night he jerked awake, feeling bloated. Grabbing his flashlight, he went out to ease himself, but no matter how he shone the beam at his piss, it looked no different to usual. He couldn't get back to sleep after that, and finally he decided to ignore Grandpa Li's warning and gulped down the other half. At least this little bug could have its two halves reunited. It didn't feel good, being apart from Blossom.

In the morning, he was the first to get up. He went for another pee. It came out very hot, but without a drop of red. He broke into a frantic sweat. What if these bugs didn't work?

All day long, he stayed near the urn and kept drinking hot water, cup after cup, but during the many resultant trips to the lavatory, the liquid gushing out of him was completely clear. He got the jar out for another look. The shriveled black bugs glared as if they wanted to eat him.

"What rubbish, only eat half at a time. I had a whole one, and my piss is still just piss!"

That night, he waited till the others were sound asleep, then gulped down another blister beetle. This time it wasn't just crawling but flying around inside him, flitting here and there till he dropped off. No dreams that night. In the morning, he rose and went to the toilet, and when the piss shot out of him it burnt like fire. He looked down and saw red threaded through the yellow stream. He forced himself to stop, went back to the dorm for a beer bottle, collected the rest of the urine and made an appointment at the clinic.

Dr. Ma, the internist, took his pulse, pressed a stethoscope to his chest his back his belly, then glanced at his tongue and flicked back his eyelids. After these rituals, he asked what was wrong? (Shouldn't *he* be asking the doctor that?)

"Fever, blood in the urine." He held up the beer bottle. Dr. Ma misunderstood.

"From drinking too much?"

"No, this is piss, and there's blood in it." He brandished the bottle very earnestly.

Dr. Ma's head reared and he held his breath as he scribbled a note to the lab.

Horseface was at the lab counter that day. He handed over the beer bottle.

"What's this?"

"Piss."

"Whose?"

"Mine."

"This won't do! You can't urinate before we ask you to. This could belong to anyone!"

Horseface? More like the horse-headed demon guarding the gates of Hell. He thought of the two beetles he'd swallowed, and gently felt his crotch. No problem! The burning sensation was still there. "Then I'll pee right here in front of you."

"Ruffian!" The corner of her lip twitched flirtatiously, and she summoned Old Li.

"Old Li! Follow this educated youth and watch him urinate. Director's orders. Medical discharges have to be handled carefully."

The elderly odd-job man nodded.

In the toilet, with Old Li staring at his thingy, he couldn't force anything out.

"Could you stop looking? What's there to look at?"

"I have to. Director called a special meeting yesterday. No sending good people home, no misdiagnosing bad people."

He pushed in his stomach, but still no piss emerged. Old Li swallowed and walked to the sink to turn on the faucet, looking back at him. As soon as the water started flowing, so did his piss. He watched the stream carefully and grew less anxious when he saw there was still red in it. He handed the little bottle to Old Li, who carried it off like a sacrificial offering.

The lab report came back with four plus signs. "What poisonous little creatures, just two of them wrecked a big fellow like me," he thought.

Four plus signs made him feel he really was ill.

He hobbled into the internist's office, one hand supporting his back. Dr. Ma was sipping tea. He placed the report on the desk. Dr. Ma looked at the four plus signs, and the teacup in his hand trembled. He took our guy's pulse again and murmured, "Powerful stuff!" Sweat broke out across his brow—he'd thought for a moment the doctor was referring to the beetles. Next came the prescription.

He sat there, not moving, until Dr. Ma looked up to urge him to go get his medicine. "Doctor, give me a diagnosis."

"I can't do that now, but I'll give you a week's bed rest."

"Never mind the bed rest, give me a diagnosis. There aren't any proper hospitals here, and no medicine to be had either. I want to go back to Shanghai to be cured."

"Finish this course of pills, then we'll see."

Dr. Ma picked up his teacup in dismissal. Our guy banged the beer bottle on the desk.

"Look! There's blood in this piss. And you just said, 'Powerful stuff!' Chairman Mao tells us to help the ill and wounded, to fulfill the humanist principles of Revolution."

The bottle of urine sat on the table. It was a long time before Dr. Ma was able to swallow his mouthful of tea. When he'd forced it down, he pulled out a drawer and wrote out a diagnosis of acute kidney inflammation.

Our guy stood up and thanked him, then walked out of his office, leaving the piss bottle.

Finally, a medical discharge.

The day he left, Lion Snout sent him off at the train station. Before going, he pulled the jar from his pocket and handed it over.

"For kidney inflammation. Take one at night, and you'll be pissing blood the next day. Don't take more than one at a time."

Lion Snout stared at the bugs and tears slowly crept from his eyes, perhaps from gratitude, perhaps because he was sad to see his friend go.

The train started. He still hadn't told anyone about bouncing the mercury to one end of the thermometer. He'd come up with that trick himself—it couldn't be passed on lightly.

LIGHTNING ROD

When a group of people need to fritter away unwanted time, the best method is gambling.

How you do this depends on the time and place. It can happen anywhere: at mealtimes, dare someone to eat fifteen steamed buns; walking down the street, bet on whether you can climb an electric pole and touch the insulation at the top; dare each other to jump over a table, leap across a ditch, light twenty fuses from a single cigarette (while blasting rocks), down a jin and a half of grain spirits (that person was flung outside into the snow afterward and spent an hour in the freezing cold sobering up). Yes, there really are a multitude of ways to gamble.

So much competition in the world, most of it captured in the *Guinness Book of World Records*, which makes the whole business seem absurdly solemn and inflexible. Bros who can quickly gulp down thirty chili peppers go down in history just like the most notable politicians. Nothing wrong with this—humanity has too many days to dispose of, and time drags on so.

Those days in the Great Northern Waste, we relied on gambling to improve the quality of mundane stretches of time. My memories of that period in my life are riddled with such episodes.

Night Cat and Miao Quan went to the well on the coldest day of the year, forty degrees below zero, and Night Cat flung his new basin down the shaft. Miao Quan's dare was to retrieve this, so he took off all his clothes and jumped in. Night Cat lost a tin of food, but also felt he'd got one over Miao Quan, whom he resented for beating him in every other area of life. He used the rescued basin as a urinal from then on, pissing into it every day.

One stormy summer day, we were in the grain store unloading provisions. One by one we came in, canvas sacks slung over our shoulders, while dark clouds gathered above us. Then all at once, a deluge of raindrops the size of copper coins, thunder like a millstone. A boom accompanied by a lightning flash, rattling the roof tiles.

Next to us was the flour factory, a three-story building with a sloping roof, and on its spine a lightning rod, the only one for a hundred li around. This metal pole stuck three fingers up at the storm, dismissing it.

Nothing to do but crouch beneath the eaves, waiting for the heavy rain to stop. Old Jian called out, "Anyone dare to climb up and grab the lightning rod? I'll stake a bottle of wine." No one paid any attention, and the thunder grew louder than before. This bet would lead to certain death, and anyone making these kinds of dares was regarded as the deadest of the deadbeats, fit only to be ignored. He shouted again, "Fine, I'll throw in another bottle." Now the crowd started yelling at him to keep going. He got up to seven bottles, but still there were no takers.

As the storm grew heavier, Night Cat dashed from the shelter toward the metal ladder of the building next door. Each time the lightning showed itself, it seemed there were two silhouettes running. He was taking the bet. We were all standing now, eyes fixed on him.

He got to the top of the ladder. The tiles were slippery, so he kicked off his shoes and flung them to the ground, walking barefoot across the slick surface. Another flash of lightning. Against its blaze, he looked suddenly tall and strong. Crouching down, he began crawling up the slope excruciatingly slowly as water sluiced past him.

Everyone was watching, afraid he'd get washed down before reaching the top. Miao Quan cried out, "Come back! You win!" But his voice was swallowed by the rain. We all shouted together, "You win the bet!"

Night Cat inched his way to the highest point of the roof just as the loudest thunderclap boomed, and in the blink of an eye he had vanished. There was no one to be seen against the skyline. Miao Quan wept, "Damn you, we said you'd won, why'd you have to go and do that!"

The storm was at its height now, and in the near-darkness, Night Cat pulled himself up from the tiles. He'd only slipped, not fallen. One step at a time, he dragged himself to the lightning rod and wrapped a hand around it, using it to haul himself to a standing position. The wind and rain swirled around him as black clouds scudded overhead. More thunder exploded from the sky, and lightning outlined his figure.

Victorious, Night Cat looked down at us and called, "Seen enough?" We all screamed back, "Yes! That's enough!" He took one last look at the sky, savoring his moment as a conquering hero, before reluctantly heading back down.

We shared the seven bottles between us, and everyone got thoroughly drunk. Night Cat didn't touch a single drop. Alcohol couldn't match the intoxication of his moment on the roof.

FIRST HARVEST

When I was in the Sixth Propaganda Brigade, we had a performance called "Harvest Dance." Six girls appeared with yellow satin ribbons in their left hands and prop sickles in their right, going through the motions of harvesting wheat on stage, joyous and light. These fake farmers never stopped smiling as they scythed and gathered. I was in the orchestra, and in order to replicate the experience, I pressed the bow down hard on my violin, but every time I did that, my fellow musicians complained. I guess the difference is I'd harvested wheat before, and they never had.

When we got to the Great Northern Waste in 1969, it was already the middle of August, yet the wheat was still moldering in the ground. Autumn rains had made the soil impassable to tractors, so the crop continued to ripen, like children who couldn't go home. There was a slogan at the time, "snatching food from the dragon's mouth," which I found very stirring. It had exactly the right combination of myth and fighting spirit to appeal to a seventeen-year-old.

The sickles we were issued were the simple, northern kind. We grabbed one each and did what the locals did: spat on a stone and started whetting. The sharpened blade felt cold when we tested it against a fingernail, and with a single sweep, we left piles of flattened grass next to us. This added to the sense of heroism—young people hard at work accomplishing things.

It was still raining when we set off. My classmates had their own raincoats in all sorts of designs, mostly pale-colored ones, bestowed by their parents. The hats were even worse—baseball caps and an assortment of army headgear—which made our little harvest troop look somewhat wishy-washy.

People who haven't been to the Great Northern Waste don't have a clear sense of the land—they tend to think of it as if seen from above, a flat surface ready to be sliced into squares. It was different here. There were areas it took a whole day to get to and back on a tractor. Harvesting wheat in such a vast space? Our sickles suddenly felt tiny and insignificant. Looking at the croplands that seemed to fill the entire heaven and earth, we didn't know where to start. Our leader called out: Six rows per person, six rows per person . . . And pushed everyone with a sickle to the front line. Next to me was the Little Mute (he wasn't actually mute but had a speech impediment that made him hard to understand), dressed more like a businessman who'd fallen on hard times. The edge of his raincoat was caked in mud, and his baseball cap was too big—it fell over his eyes whenever he raised or lowered his head.

By the time we actually started work, the pride with which we'd scythed the grass had completely evaporated. The only way to get the waterlogged wheat out of the ground was a combination of hacking and tugging. I'd only gotten ten meters before my legs sank completely into the ground. The wheat floated on this soup of earth, waiting to be scooped up rather than harvested. The rain got heavier, and soon the entire troop was waist deep in mud. One by one, the rice-colored raincoats turned around, looking to our leader. Similarly engulfed, he made a gesture and quietly said, "Let's pack up." We crawled out and retreated, leaving our meager haul of wheat to be swallowed by the flood.

We'd been roundly defeated by mud. All the way home, I found myself thinking about the Battle of Waterloo.

For the month after that, we continued harvesting Seventh Field.

It stopped raining, and the land eventually dried. A few hundred of us worked away on the infinite earth. Now and then we'd straighten our backs and look at the distant hills. The croplands stretched all the way over there. When would we ever reach the edge?

In the first few days, quite a few people suffered cuts to their arms and legs. I stopped sharpening my blade, advanced with a sort of chopping motion and managed to get away uninjured thanks to my old fur-lined leather boots, which fended off many sneak attacks. By the end of the month, only two of the thirty-odd group were still harvesting: me and another person.

Exhaustion was normal, but thirst was harder to withstand. The team bringing us water had a long way to come, and half of it sloshed out along the way. If you weren't quick enough, you'd get to the bucket only to find it empty. Nothing worse than an empty bucket—it made you feel all the more parched.

Finally, we discovered a foot or so of water had accumulated at the lowest point of the land. Pond scum and mayflies covered the surface of these puddles, and though I tried several times, I couldn't bring myself to drink from them. In the end, Lion Snout came up with a method: blowing through a wheat stalk to clear its hollow center, then using it as a straw to sip the clear water beneath the green stuff and bugs, as elegantly as if he were back in Beijing drinking Arctic Ocean soda. When he was done, he let out an exaggerated sigh of contentment, exactly like someone enjoying a cold beverage at the height of summer. We all rushed to copy him. After every boy in Three-Three had had their fill, the puddle was drained. In the end, Lion Snout was the only one who got sick, while the rest of us carried on as before. It's not easy being a pioneer, you have to make sacrifices.

Because we were so far from base, lunch got delivered to us. Most of us didn't have watches, so we relied on our stomachs to tell the time. When we got hungry, we kept pausing our scything to look behind us, and when we saw the oxcart arriving, we'd put down the tools right away. Nothing was more exhilarating then rushing head-long toward food. I was later reminded of this sight, a whole field of people running in a pack, when I saw the start of a marathon years later. All of us sprinting to the same place, full of energy. We'd get to the truck and all hands would grab as much as possible. I usually had about seven packets, though one time I managed nine (they were about two liang each), which was still average. Lion Snout had twelve.

There was a break after lunch, so we'd pile the harvested wheat into giant, soft mattresses that we lounged on, dozing in the autumn sun and watching little insects hop around. Our only desire was not to pick up our sickles, to never face the borderless land again.

It was during this time that I saw a mole (locally known as a "blind pestle") for the first time. As I lay drowsing, it popped up from the earth like a wandering spirit, staring at me through half-shut eyes. It scurried over to my battered shoes and gnawed at my laces, a sweet sensation, like being nibbled at, though I worried it would squeeze through a hole and find my stinky toes.

After a month, although we still hadn't gathered all the crops, the soil was dry enough for tractors to take over, and we could pack away our tools. We looked at one another, tanned dark and filthy, infested with fleas. Most of us had taken up smoking—Economy brand cigarettes were nine cents a pack, a single one made you cough non-stop. Everyone quietly shed tears when they got their first letter from home. On October 1, we listened to the National Day celebrations from Beijing, while a snowstorm rose outside the window.

THE HAIR

Nothing mattered now. I waited for his fingers to move.

Smoke came from his mouth, insinuating itself between us and lingering there. I'd spread my cards: three kings and a pair of tens, a "full house" as they say in English. Sturdy-sounding, like a zodiac sign or a fortress. Next to this fortress was my last hundred and twenty yuan and a Shanghai brand watch. His fingers wriggled over the cards like sea serpents, rearranging the face-up jack, queen, ten, and nine. Finally, he lifted his hole card from behind the queen, carefully studied it, and turned it over. A king. His sword slashed through the air, drawing blood from my heart that spattered into my eyes and made everything blurry.

He took my cash, held my watch up to his ear, then strapped it to his left wrist, next to the thirteen others. His left arm was encased in metal like armor, and it was a struggle to fit mine on. These watches were like prisoners standing stiffly in a line, time clinking against itself whenever he moved his arm. The cloud of smoke sank, revealing his face, a wilderness with a lush growth of exhaustion. The voice that sprang from among those weeds was hoarse and cracked.

"You're out again."

I stood, grabbed my leather cap and left the room full of smoke and eyes.

It was strangely cold outside. The night drew me like a magnet, but when I sank into it, the darkness grew impossibly distant. There were no shadows on the ground as I walked lightly along. Time was now on someone else's arm.

*

On a night like this one, I went with him to Fifth Brigade. I'd cobbled together thirty yuan (a month's wages) and he said that was enough. Snow crunched underfoot like broken glass. When we got close to the courtyard a dog barked, heart-clenchingly loud. He rattled the bamboo gate and called out. After a long time, someone in a fur hat came to let us in. I whispered in his ear, "Let's just make two hundred, enough to get home. Don't get carried away." Acting as though he hadn't heard, he followed Fur Hat into the building.

The room reeked of stale pickled vegetables. All the bedding on the scorching hot kang platform had been rolled to one side. He and I sat on a deerskin each, like messengers or army generals riding into battle. The cards were shuffled. Opposite Fur Hat was a man with a glass eye that glistened and seemed fixated on my shirt button. Glass Eye partnered with my friend, while Fur Hat and I took turns to deal. After the first round, Glass Eye turned over the ace of spades and put down ten yuan. My friend showed the ten of clubs and also tossed in ten yuan. By the third round, Glass Eye had two aces face-up and twenty yuan on the table. He drew another card, glanced at it and folded.

We won twenty yuan on the next hand. My friend put down the stake gingerly, knowing exactly how little we had left.

At three in the morning, by which time I estimated he'd won about three hundred yuan, he left the small bills out, put all the tens into his hat, and placed the hat on his head.

Glass Eye's glass eye stared dispassionately, tirelessly fastened to my shirt button. My friend took money from his shirt pocket like open-heart surgery, and it clung to his fingers a long time before he put it down. I shot him many glances urging him to leave, but he looked at his cards in silence and put more money down, fingers spreading elegantly, ignoring me.

Glass Eye turned over a pair of kings and pair of jacks. With three tens and an ace face up, my friend threw in a hundred and fifty yuan. Sweat poured down Glass Eye's face like tears. I know he had a full house: three kings and a pair of jacks. My friend definitely didn't have a fourth ten—his hole card was an eight, which I'd dealt him that first round. Glass Eye's sweat spattered on the hot kang and fizzled into steam, and his right hand remained pressed to his chest. My friend calmly puffed on a cigarette, his face a distant mountain behind the smoke. Glass Eye shut his good eye, allowing the glass one to survey the room, except it remained fixed to my button. My heart was being pierced by countless arrows. Fur Hat took off his fur hat. His head was glowing red.

Glass Eye's right hand came out, empty, and he turned his cards face down.

My friend took the money and stacked his cards, passing them to me.

We played two more hands. My friend lost a little over thirty yuan, then stood and said he needed the bathroom. The rules of gambling were that the loser got to decide when you stopped, unless you'd agreed on a time beforehand. My friend put on his hat and walked out the door, leaving some small bills scattered on the table.

Glass Eye finally swiveled to face me. His real eye was clear as a lake in autumn, and I thought I could see all the way to the bottom. A beautiful eye, long lashes holding many words, far too lucid to be the eye of a gambler. Yet something blazed in it too, a bonfire by a lake.

We waited twenty minutes, but the door didn't open again.

I eased myself off the deer skin and stood up.

"I'll go look for him—maybe he fell into the shit pit," I said to

Glass Eye. The lake turned toward me. The fire had grown into an inferno, and now it swung toward Fur Hat.

"I'll go with you." Fur Hat put on his hat and walked me out the door.

The night was enchantingly light. I looked up at the stars. My breath showed up in puffs of white, giving a form to my panting.

Fur Hat stayed two paces away from me. He'd picked up a shovel, which made my situation somewhat more valorous. I went through the gate and pissed by a pile of straw, gouging a yellow hole in the snow. My chest suddenly felt empty, as if all the dirty air inside me had been expelled.

When I turned around, my friend had his blade pressed to Fur Hat's back.

"Go back in and tell Glass Eye I got tired of playing. I'll come again another day. Keep this fifty for yourself." He pulled five notes from his hat and stuck them into Fur Hat's collar.

"Don't just go like that. Kick my ass. He'll need to see blood." Fur Hat turned around to let my friend stab him, then hobbled back through the gate.

All the way back to our brigade, he stared at the flying snow. I couldn't tear my eyes away from the stars—which of them was over my distant hometown, and the thing known as family? The next morning, my friend gave me five hundred yuan so I could take my granny to see a doctor. On my way back, he said, I should bring a few more decks of cards.

*

Nighttime—when you experience her freshness, her fragrance and moods, the stars dotted around and wisps of cloud like hair, the mysterious, vast space when the moon is absent, you feel you have nothing you can rely on. When you can't sense her, she seems ancient, immutable as steel. The sounds you hear are auditory hallucinations within her. Now you can walk with your eyes shut back to your bunk and lie down. By the time you fall asleep, the night has shrunk to the tiny darkness behind your eyelids.

For two years he'd played cards non-stop, his fingers growing longer and longer. They looked like a musician's when he spread them, the tips thick with sensitivity and sorrow, the fingerprints full of eyes. He felt like a presence lurking in the fog, reaching out so you emptied your pockets and placed all your money in his hands.

I'd hoped to win some money so I could go home the next day, but instead I'd lost it all, including the watch that ought to have accompanied me all my life.

When I went again the next day, I found Lion Snout hard at it with him. Lion Snout had three jacks, while he had three kings. He glanced at the pile of banknotes in front of Lion Snout, and tossed out two hundred yuan. Lion Snout sat in silence for a very long time, looking at his hole card three times. It was a jack. He counted his money: a hundred and sixty, not enough. His opponent sat spewing smoke from his mouth, blowing it up into his face. He was dependable like that: no matter the time of day, he'd be a fixture there. Whether the cards went his way or not, his expression never changed. He'd probably worked out that Lion Snout had four jacks, but no one could guess whether his own fourth card was a king. Lion Snout put all his money on the table, and when he didn't react, took off his sweater and put it on top of the cash, then turned over the hole card. His opponent looked at the four jacks, put his own hole card down, and flipped it over to show a king. He took all the money and pulled the sweater over his head. As his arm moved, I caught a glimpse of my watch, or his watch now I guess.

For the next few days, I sat by the side of the table, taking over for the dealer. Almost immediately, I knew for certain he wasn't cheating. He seemed to have the ability to unerringly sense his opponent's hole card, while his own remained firmly face down—he hardly ever touched it. At crucial moments, he raised his stake high enough to crush them. I often found myself sweating on his behalf, because I knew for a fact he was bluffing.

On the fourth day, I finally discovered a little secret—a tiny one, so small no one else would have noticed it, not even himself. I spent the fifth day confirming my theory. On day six, I borrowed some money and arrived at the table early to wait for him, trying to look calm and unagitated. He arrived and I stared at his face; nothing had changed. The mole on his scrawny chin, and the hair sprouting from that mole, were still there.

After three rounds, I'd assembled a seriously good full house: three tens and two jacks. His face cards were a pair of jacks and a pair of queens. When it came time to raise, he tried to crush me right away by looking at the pile of money in front of me and putting down a hundred and fifty. I looked blankly at the cards in front of me, then after some time, looked up at the hair on his mole. This was his little secret: through the smoke, I glimpsed it quivering. You had to hold your breath to see this, like a tiny stalk of grass in the wind, lonely and trembling with fear. I counted out a hundred and fifty and put it out. He lost—all he had was a lowly nine. He stared in puzzlement at the cards and stubbed out a cigarette he'd just lit.

On the seventh hand, he tried again to intimidate me by betting two hundred yuan and a watch. I studied our hands, eyed the pile of money in front of me, and once again looked to his face for an answer. He'd always been skinny, and lived mainly on tobacco, though unlike most smokers, his skin was pale and lustrous as jade. The mole was on his cliff-like jaw. I looked at the cliff and found the hair perfectly still. He waited. Smoke drifted past the gaudy playing cards, then dispersed. I folded without raising once. He came away empty-handed.

He lost more times that day than he had for several years. During our last hand, he removed the final three watches from his left arm, one of them mine. The hair twitched again, just a little, but my eye caught it. I showed my cards and scooped up everything on the table. When we ended the game, I had seven watches on my arm, and time was startlingly loud. I tossed a couple of notes to Sharpie, who'd been keeping an eye on the cards, and returned Lion Snout the money I'd borrowed. Just before I left, I glanced at his face again, and for once it was red. Like an unexpectedly glimpsed sunset, this was a melancholy sight.

"You beat me today." Still that dry voice, seeming to emanate from the burning cigarette.

"See you tomorrow!"

"See you tomorrow!"

That night, I spent a long time unable to sleep because of that hair. The way it trembled made me so happy. He was no iceberg, he'd just managed to bury his anxiety deep underground, like a hidden river beneath the surface of his skin. Yet his own hair betrayed him. My only fear was: What if he cut it off? But no, for the next three days, the hair brought me victory after victory. He melted away. I had more than twenty watches, which I wore on both arms. Time had wrapped itself tightly around me, drowning out my pulse.

Someone told me he'd been trying to borrow money everywhere, but no one was willing to lend. He'd spent the last two years beating everyone, and now it seemed he was providing them with entertainment. On the fourth day, he told me he'd lost everything.

"You've wiped me out."

Before going, he touched the cards one last time. His hand was pale as light, brushing across them. He seemed to shrink as he walked away. I thought about the time he'd taken me gambling to make me the money for a trip home and almost called after him to cut off the hair, but I stopped myself.

These four days had brought me no excitement. Every round felt like guessing riddles I already knew the answer to. Just like tending to my crops, only the harvest was cash or clothes or watches. I sold the watches and sweaters back to their owners for token amounts. In exchange for his own watch, he gave me a picture—Vasily Surikov's *Morning of the Streltsy Execution*—which used to hang by his bed.

FALSE COLLAR

The orchestra was in tune, their scores at the ready before them. The choir filed onto their risers, while the stage manager stood at the center to ensure that everything was in order, then signaled for the curtain to rise and lights to come on overhead and in front of us. Now it was too late to change anything.

The conductor strode to his position and took his bow. Standing on his little podium, he solemnly surveyed his forces, then raised an arm and we were off! The overture commenced: the trumpets half a beat behind, the cellos flat. With slightly wrinkled brow and energetic gestures, he expressed dissatisfaction then pleasure when the kettledrum (substituting for a flowerpot drum) entered on time, and the tuba executed a splendid, resonant phrase. The conductor flung himself into his work, moving as he believed maestros should, body bent forward, wrists high, attention focused on the string section. Then his hands came together and apart dramatically, like a chef pulling noodles, the breadth of his gestures leading the musicians along. In the stillness of a woodwind passage, the choir and strings swept in. With that, the conductor abandoned the orchestra and turned his agitated face to the singers, communing with them, projecting all the energy he could muster, trying to elicit a more spirited performance. His mouth held the right emotions, opening and shutting correctly, but anyone could see he wasn't making a sound, like an impostor trying to look the part. He wanted the high voices to make a brighter sound, a little brighter. His left hand swept up, and up again, but it was no good, you couldn't expect these fellows to abruptly become masters of the high Cs. Besides, where would they find the energy? You had nothing to feed them, and your own last meal had only been potatoes and cabbage.

The first song drew to a close, the audience applauded, and the conductor turned to bow. As he straightened up, his false collar came undone, half of it reaching up to paw at his cheek, the other remaining tucked into his jacket. This triggered some disorder in the next song; his stern demeanor and that fake, twisted collar presented a stark contrast. As his arms moved vigorously, a patch of white bobbed before his face. During a particularly intoxicating, lyrical passage, a soprano lost control and let out a giggle. That was the breach in the dam—laughter being the most contagious thing on stage—and we couldn't stop it exploding across the company. His sternness and fury only exacerbated our frenzy. The choir infected the musicians, and soon everyone was in hysterics. Hastily the curtain came down.

This was one of our more disastrous performances during my time in the Great Northern Waste. It was an important one too, meant to welcome a senior official. Nowadays we'd just write off the concert as a bust, but back then it had to be treated as a political issue. The next day, everyone who'd laughed on stage sat and wept as they self-criticized. Nobody blamed the false collar; we found fault only with ourselves. As for the conductor, Shanghai Zheng, he swore that at all future performances he'd go on stage with a bare neck. He'd rather reveal his somewhat grubby but sturdy neck than wrap it in an inauthentic garment, and risk political mockery should this scrap of white cloth go awry.

It was only after moving to the Great Northern Waste that I encountered false collars. They first became fashionable among the educated youths of Shanghai—round ones, pointy ones, patterned ones. Girls put on a different one every day, a pageant as extravagant as any princess. Yet observing these people with their false collars, I could think only of what was missing underneath. To begin with, I'd thought the collars meant principally that you lacked a complete shirt. Later, I discovered their actual function—as a barrier between cotton undershirt and wool overshirt. Our cotton shirts had no collar, and adding a false one prevented the woolen top layer from chafing against the neck.

False collars grew more popular, and lots of people began sporting them. The wearers generally fell into two groups: those who wore them for their appearance, usually only on important occasions, and those who valued their tiny practical function.

As I owned a collared shirt, I never needed to wear a false collar during performances, nor was I worried about woolen garments scratching my neck. In any case, my entire body was covered in flea bites and there was no way I could have passed myself off as a civilized human being.

More than a decade later, this item of clothing came vividly to mind. I was reluctantly listening to the editor of a publishing house make a hypocritical speech. His lies, so vigorously and expansively delivered, recalled the debacle of that false collar. If I'd been wearing one at that moment, rather than saying a word, I'd simply have opened my jacket casually and revealed the false collar to the speaker, showing it off from all angles. Look at this, it's false, a false collar. This would be the most splendid performance of any false collar, because only at that moment would it become real.

But that wasn't possible. The times have changed, and I'm a civilized human being now. I've gotten used to being a phony.

BELCH

Old Yoo played the round horn, which he called the "French horn," in the propaganda orchestra. When he followed the score, his grasp of rhythm was exceptionally accurate. Old Yoo usually didn't practice very much. One time the political commissar overheard him rehearsing and called the little tune he was playing "the stinking fart of the bourgeoisie." This saddened Old Yoo. He put away his horn and asked Old Qian to teach him the erhu. He learned to read simple notation and to play *Waters of the Yangtze and Yellow Rivers*. The commissar listened to his rendition and commented that Old Yoo had improved in his thinking.

The full name of our brigade was "Mao Zedong Thought Propaganda Orchestra." Apart from our own little concerts, we mostly staged revolutionary operas. Being short-staffed, each performer often took on three or four roles each. In *Legend of the Red Lantern*, I played a liaison officer, a spy, and one of the Japanese devils at the execution ground. In addition, I operated the curtain and special effects.

Old Yoo kept to the orchestra, playing both the round horn and erhu, and was also the electrician in charge of the loading platform. He most enjoyed the horn solo in *Taking Tiger Mountain*. He even received a round of applause at one performance, and for ages afterward sat clutching his instrument in a daze.

He compared the tone of the round horn to "white clouds above a palace." What did he think of the oboe? "A girl by the water." And the clarinet? "A young guy growing his first beard." So what about the erhu? He thought about it and whispered, "The whining of the political commissar's wife."

Old Yoo met his girlfriend when he was twenty-six. She was a Shanghai educated youth from the brickworks named Blossom, a scrawny thing who spoke in her city's dialect, bringing to mind old-time Shanghai actresses like Zhou Xuan and Ruan Lingyu. Each night, Old Yoo walked twenty li to meet her at the brick factory. Before setting out, he'd say, I'm going to do it with her tonight. When he got back we'd ask, Did you do it? And he'd say no—there was always someone working late at the kiln. We'd ask if he was tired from the forty-li round trip, and he'd say, Of course I'm exhausted, brain and body both. Luckily I can catch a cab back—a ride in the cab of the brick van, that is!

One night, he came back badly injured. The van had overturned into a ditch, and he'd been battered by falling bricks. He ended up in the hospital with a broken leg. When we visited, he was miserable. Blossom had just left, having told him in Mandarin that it was over between them. Old Yoo asked me why she'd switched to Mandarin to inflict these cruel words. I couldn't come up with a reason. Perhaps she felt it was more solemn, more proper. Old Yoo spat out "Bitch," then mysteriously informed me it was just as well, she had women's issues.

After Old Yoo was discharged, he had a bit of a limp, though you wouldn't notice unless you were looking closely. He kept up a front of nonchalance, but withdrew into himself, not bathing or washing his clothes for months at a time, then finally taking to drink. Playing while drunk chapped his lips, but he pressed on until a layer of calloused skin formed.

One time we performed for the armed forces. The People's Liberation Army was always particularly welcoming. After we set up the stage, they offered us all a drink. Afraid of fumbling during the performance, everyone declined—apart from Old Yoo. As he drank, he toasted, "Liquor brings soldiers and the People together, like family." We thought he was knocking back too many and advised him to slow down. He said he was fine.

The performance started and everyone got swept up, including Old Yoo, who was switching frantically between horn and erhu. When we reached *Taking Tiger Mountain*, he clutched the horn to his chest, pressed down on the valves, and entered on the right beat. But halfway through the passage, Old Yoo suddenly stopped and let out an enormous belch, loud and resonant. We were shocked for a moment but couldn't help laughing. With the orchestra in hysterics, the music grew unsteady. Waiting in the wings, the actor playing Yang Zirong missed the cues for both his entrance and his aria. The show descended into chaos, and finally we were forced to bring the curtain down and start over.

Right after the performance, the political commissar held a meeting that lasted through the night. He said Old Yoo had let out an "anti-revolutionary belch." After this, Old Yoo gave up the round horn. We replaced all the horn passages with the cello, while he stuck to the erhu and operating the electricity.

I thought of Old Yoo again yesterday. I asked my wife if she remembered him and she said she did, but he was called Old Yew, not Old Yoo. Still I can't bring myself to change it. I can't explain why, but I feel like if I were to use his correct name, I wouldn't recognize him anymore.

THROUGH

Of all the strange dreams I've had, none of them involved death. Expiring, tasting death, then waking up—nothing like that. Perhaps death is too serious a matter to bring into a dream. I've asked around, and other people tell me the same thing. Death never enters their dreams.

I've seen death—pale, cold, and bloodless. Like the words suddenly vanishing from a book, leaving blank paper, page after page of it. Such a death would make even the sunniest day blink, exhausted. Right in front of you. A wind rises, as if blowing from your heart.

1.

They got on the truck at Third Division, Tenth Brigade. The woman clutched a bundle to her chest, a baby, crying softly. The man was grubby, well-built, a cigarette butt drooping from his lips. It was freezing, so we passed a small bottle of baijiu sorghum liquor around the truck. Spirits in icy weather chill the teeth, only warming up in your belly. I thought of passing the bottle to the man, then noticed his cold-stiffened hands were busy rolling a fresh cigarette.

The four of us had been sent to the depot for more noodles—our brigade had run out, so breakfast that day consisted of potatoes and soybeans, mashed together with strips of pickled vegetables. Everyone in the canteen complained this was no better than pig swill.

By the time the bottle came round a second time, there were only a few drops left. This is when alcohol is most fragrant, barely dribbling into your mouth, the faint aroma melting, dispersing before you can even swallow it, your mouth yearning for more, but all you can do is shake the empty container. The taste lingers a long time on your tongue.

The man finished rolling his cigarette. He turned to one side to light it, then swung back, an expert move: twisting away from the wind to light up, facing it to smoke. He was enjoying the flavor, holding it in his mouth a long time before expelling a plume of smoke, eyes squinting shut.

It was so cold we were unwilling to pee, afraid losing that tiny amount of heat would leave us frozen through. Old Ta'er said people who freeze to death don't have any piss left in them. You feel as if your body's on fire, blazing with pain. Old Ta'er had the right to tell us things like that—he'd lost both legs to frostbite.

The bundle that was the baby had been quiet a long time.

In lieu of the crying baby, the woman was sobbing silently, head lowered. Tears dripped onto the front of her jacket, instantly freezing into little crystals. What was there to cry about?

The man's cigarette went out, another long butt dangling from his lips, as if he hadn't noticed anything at all.

As we went over Eastern Hill, a few roe deer ran out, frolicking like it was springtime.

The woman was sobbing audibly now, shoulders heaving.

The man spat out his cigarette.

"Why bother crying? So it's dead, we'll make another one." She kept weeping. He rolled another cigarette.

"Stop it, hey, you'll get wrinkles."

What was dead? The child? Surely not, it was howling just a short while ago. Why not open the bundle? Maybe it's only sleeping.

A tiny face, pale and translucent as paper, eyes screwed up, not a single sound. I touched a cheek and found it cold, a jade pebble in the snow. Lion Snout put his hand to its mouth.

Dead. Just two months old. Why bring it outside, on a day like this?

The baby had been sick. Fever all night. The man rolled another cigarette.

Maybe it had just fainted. The brigade hospital might be able to—No. Just another child. What could they do with it, even alive?

The woman stopped crying and wrapped the bundle loosely. A mother holding her own child's corpse has such sorrow on her face, she seems more distant than the stars.

Death comes so quickly. A few mouthfuls of spirits, one cigarette, and a child is gone, like a bright flash of light. The jade pebble I'd just felt was death. A snowflake landed on my fingertip and melted.

It had been living, now it was dead. No different to the blanket it was wrapped in. No crying, not a sound, neither cold nor hot anymore.

The four of us tucked our heads in, and the cold between us was greater than a piece of ice. We were just seventeen and had never seen death. I felt we should do something for the child in the bundle. Weep, or take turns to keep it warm until it woke.

At the depot, the couple walked away, and we went to pick up our noodles.

There'd been a power outage. They didn't have a single bag of noodles for us.

We browsed the shops instead and watched the couple from a distance. The woman wasn't holding her bundle any longer. She was at the counter, choosing a piece of patterned fabric, like the other ladies around her. Picking up a length of cloth, she studied it intently, then held it up against her chest where her child had been earlier, where her tears had frozen solid.

How dazzling that pattern was.

We retreated. So quickly. The wind was still howling, but where was the child? It might as well never have existed.

2.

One time Sharpie had an allergic reaction to sulfur and was admitted to the brigade hospital. It was summer, and he was covered in a rash. Looking like a piece of coarse sandpaper spread out across the bed, he whispered to me that it was worst in his private parts. He said if he wasn't afraid of death, he'd never have come here. At night a multitude of bedbugs attacked him, causing swelling on top of his rash, leaving him covered in different varieties of itches. When he touched his skin, it felt like his, but also like someone else's. And there's—Sharpie's eyes darted to the patient in the next bed—he's about to die, his stomach's all rotten, it's his intestines, he hasn't eaten anything for a long time. You smell that, like a pickling vat? Sometimes I wake up and I don't know where I am, it's frightening, goddammit I'm so scared.

The other patient's head poked out from under a filthy blanket. I'd never seen anyone so thin, just hair and skin. His eyes were shut. He was so still he could have been a shadow.

An educated youth?

No, he's just sixteen.

No family?

Didn't you see the guys gambling in the corridor as you came in? His brothers and uncles.

Don't they care about him?

They look in on him every now and again, then they go back out.

Last night, I woke up and saw him staring out the window, his eyes as still as water. The way he looked would break your heart. I went outside to fetch his brother. Asked what he wanted, but he said nothing, just shut his eyes. Only sixteen and already working for his family, until the illness stopped that.

The other patient woke up and looked around. I walked over and watched as his mouth opened, but his voice was thin as silk thread. I bent over to hear him say, "Open the door." At least that's what it sounded like. I told Sharpie, He said, "Open the door." Sharpie said, Go fetch his brothers and uncles. The other guy opened his mouth again, a bit louder this time. "Is Chrysanthemum here?" Or something like that. Not knowing what to say, I went out into the corridor to find the four farmers.

They'd just finished playing a hand. One of them was shuffling, the others rolling cigarettes. He's awake, I said. They kept rolling their cigarettes, but otherwise didn't budge. I said, He asked, "Is Chrysanthemum here?" One of the younger men muttered something, stood, and went into the room. The others started smoking, sorting out the piles of matchsticks in front of them—probably gambling chips.

I guess he's pretty seriously ill.

It's bad, but he's not dying.

You mean he might live?

He's not dying.

I wanted to ask who Chrysanthemum was, but didn't. My eyes and ears were still full of that young man, his wisps of words, their desolation.

The next morning, I went to see Sharpie again. The four farmers were standing in the corridor, and the other bed was empty. Sharpie said he'd died at four in the morning, or maybe three. He went easily, like a piece of ice melting while you weren't paying attention. No different to when he was alive. Death found no obstacles in his body, and in an instant, or perhaps not even that, walked across like it was level ground. His last words were, "It's still dark." He'd hoped to make it till daybreak, thinking if he could see the dawn, he'd last another day. He hadn't wanted to go but couldn't hang on. He was already cold when his uncle came in and touched him.

These last few days felt like years, said Sharpie, Watching someone die next to me, my whole goddamn worldview changed. Living feels like those ice packs the nurses bring, so cold they make you shriek. I see many things differently now. Death is terrifying because it destroys the living. But the living aren't so weak. You saw the four men outside? They're waiting to get paid. They sold the corpse.

You have to get me out of here today, no matter what. I don't dare look at that empty bed. It feels like a gateway to another place opening up right next to me. I'm so scared.

But the hospital refused to discharge Sharpie. He burst into tears, right there in front of the doctor.

3.

I went with Li Shuan to Fourth Field to gather wheat straw. Wheat straw wasn't much use: too lightweight for fuel, not worth carrying back and forth. Besides, what the combine harvester spat out was all chopped up. It was too much effort to pick up such little bits, so we set them on fire instead. After the fall, the earth blazed. Fourth Field was close to our division, so we left that alone, using the straw there to line pig pens or, mixed with mud, to insulate our huts.

Li Shuan yoked a black horse to our cart, and we headed off at eight in the morning.

He told dirty stories as he urged our horse along. Getting excited, he lashed out with the whip for emphasis. Twice he hit the horse's ears—I saw the hairs on its rump twitch with pain.

At Fourth Field, I started shoveling the hay, while Li Shuan undid his fly and pissed next to the horse. He looked east where the sun was glowing red, so warm it felt you could press your face to it. Li Shuan peed away, gilded by dawn light. There's a technique to scooping up straw with a pitchfork—get the angle wrong, and you end up without a single piece. I couldn't do it and kept coming up empty. Li Shuan fastened his trousers and said, Goddammit, you have a gun but don't know how to shoot. He came over and took the pitchfork, raking the straw into little heaps then bundling them together onto the cart. I tried to do the same while he stood in the sunlight rolling a cigarette. The black horse chewed the straw that fell by its hooves.

Thinking back, this would have made a good rustic painting—wheat, horse cart, simple labor, dawn light. The field was wide and open, and not a sound came from the distant villages.

The blind pestle (only later did I learn its proper name: a mole) emerged from the ground when the straw was half gathered, popping up right next to the horse's mouth as it chewed, startling the creature so it reared its head and galloped away. Straw scattered from my pitchfork.

Li Shuan ran after it, shouting, while straw fell off the cart in clumps. He grabbed the horse's head but was tossed off. A wheel rolled right over his belly. When I caught up, he seemed fine, though he was crying, face pale, saying his stomach hurt and he needed to pee.

I brushed the straw off him and helped him up, but he couldn't stand. He said it hurt too much, told me to go back to the division and find his mother, then come back with another cart.

When I got back with the mother and cart, Li Shuan looked like another person. He was trembling, in so much pain his features had shifted. There was no energy in him. His clothes were disheveled.

He wouldn't let anyone touch him. Even the air around him hurt. His mother crumbled a black substance into a clay bowl. Lowering herself to the ground, she cradled his head against her chest.

Drink this, it'll take the pain away.

He opened his lips and, like an infant, sipped the black broth. (Afterward, I found out it was opium.) He finished the bowl and was quiet.

His mother said, Shut your eyes and have a rest.

He said, It's so dark when I shut my eyes.

We lifted him onto our donkey cart. The sun was directly overhead.

The driver and a health worker went with him to the brigade hospital, twenty li away.

I picked up the pitchfork and broken whip handle and walked back to our division. The fields looked exactly the same as that morning. When I thought of what happened to Li Shuan, it felt like a story. Seeing the black horse made the story feel unrealistic. It had found its way back and was in its paddock chewing some grain. I lashed out at its flank with the broken whip and its hairs quivered, floating in the sunlight.

Li Shuan was brought home that night. They said he died on the way to the hospital, his liver and spleen completely crushed. There was no pain—the opium took that. His mother held him all the way. The health worker said Li Shuan's mother hadn't cried at all. She had a glass eye, but her real eye hadn't shed tears either. All she said was, You go on, wait for me up ahead.

Many years later, I saw Repin's *Ivan the Terrible and His Son Ivan* in a gallery. Looking at this overblown painting, I thought the father and son ought to swap facial expressions to be more like Li Shuan and his mother. Though one of Ivan the Terrible's eyes did look like it could be fake.

I think of these three incidents when faced with excessive grief, trying to understand why the people of the land I labored on were indifferent to death. They saw only a blurry line between life and death, as if going from one to the other was merely a journey between two places, and they saw death as only temporary, so life could be treated lightly, because we only happened to be alive right now by chance. Their hearts held a different eternity. For me, life was the only thing, all I had to cling to, and I worried it would snap off someday, like the dictionary definition of death: the loss of life. I was responsible to life alone, and time outside of this didn't exist. For a while, I lost the word "eternity," because everything was now, today was today, but tomorrow hadn't agreed it would definitely come, and the tomorrow of my imagination wasn't real anyway. I was afraid of death, and never considered I had a responsibility toward it too. Not the way religious people mean, thinking death is when our lives get inspected. What I feared was death itself, believing it to be the end of everything, so the life I'd experienced would be insignificant when weighed against death. Before this, I'd never think about whether I was worthy, so nothing I did was accountable to the end. I could leave when I wanted to. Unlike rural folk, I didn't believe in reincarnation, nor that anyone could wait up ahead for me. Had someone like me ever really lived? Would he be worth mourning?

A person has the right to death because he's lived. If you can prove you've lived, then you've earned the right to die. Death is a high honor. We talk about seeing through life and death. But that word, "through"—not many people can unravel it.

SPRINGTIME

I slumped on the ground, peering at her red face through a crack in the brick wall. The mother hen was about to lay an egg. Quietly waiting for herself.

Spring had arrived from some place. Where had it come from? A day ago, I saw a blue flower blossoming in the field, her swift blue leaving you unable to react. Only in that moment did the word "springtime" feel real.

*

When I went to hitch the horses to the cart, Old Sun was enjoying his ten o'clock tipple in the sun. He had a very thin flask he could keep in his jacket. The liquor in the flask did more to calm him than it did in his belly. When he wasn't drinking, I noticed he kept swallowing, and his hands wouldn't stop shaking.

Now he drank, and with every mouthful, he exposed the flask to sunlight. This sun-soaked liquor seemed indifferent to his fiery gaze.

I put down my reed bag and reached into its greasy depths. The reins were coiled against many random objects but had managed not to get tangled up in them. Old Sun widened an eye from behind his bottle. Amidst the bloodshot threads of red, his pupil was no longer black but like a cloud of sand grains in the wind.

The shafts were in place and secured over the back wheels. In the cart were specks of faded crimson—red crabapples, fallen from yesterday's firewood.

Old Sun picked one up and popped it into his flask. A tiny spot of red ornamenting the clear liquor.

*

I saw the cow who was about to give birth.

The draft animal named Blackflower stood in the sunlight, all alone. One of the calf's legs was protruding from her behind, like a slim oak log, soaking wet.

The cow's bellows sounded like a blunt instrument thudding against the earth.

Behind the flask, Old Sun's eyes were icy cold.

With great difficulty, the calf backed its way into the world. Its mother's trembling legs suddenly bent into a kneel, onto the straw I'd hastily heaped in front of her. I felt like she might die, her and the calf both. I tugged at the rope threaded through her nose to try to make her stand again, and tears welled in her eyes.

Springtime arrives so cruelly.

*

Old Sun brought the flask to his mouth and drained the last mouthful. Now it held nothing but the red crabapple, much larger after its soak.

He unwound the rope from around his waist and fastened it to the calf's rear leg. Pressing his own foot to the cow's rear, he pulled hard. The liquor now oozed out as sweat on his face, and his eyes were open wide.

All of a sudden, the calf gushed out like water, splashing onto the ground. A living calf, wet all over, and the placenta after it. No sooner had it hit the ground than it wanted to stand.

Old Sun was pale from exhaustion, and his hand trembled around the flask. Not a drop of liquor left. He stared at the crimson crabapple and tried to tip it into his mouth, but it rolled back and forth, refusing to come out. He picked a stalk of wheat and tried to hook it.

Finally, the tiny fruit was in his mouth. I wonder what it tasted like, as he chewed.

Springtime . . .

I was reminded of this incident yesterday, when I read a poem by Sergei Yesenin. The final stanza went:

Clouds are howling
The heavens like gold teeth scream
I sing, I pray: Lord, please calve.

I know what this poem is talking about.

LUMBER

If there'd been color at this time, I would have squeezed some purple into the freezing wind and allowed it to dapple the frosty landscape that remained unchanged for five months at a stretch. Winter was too long here. Looking at the snow stretching all the way from the horizon to your feet, a hundred determined hearts couldn't make you step out into it.

The oxcart rolled down the icy path. We clutched ourselves against the cold wind, reluctant to shift our huddled postures. A layer of sleet spattered our faces. We were truly frozen; only by getting off the cart and walking for a long time could we regain sensation in our legs.

We had run out of coal. The night before, our bedding froze to the walls, and even the thermos was icy. Cold permeated our building like an unreal wintry fairy tale.

*

The branches and trunks of the black birch would be brittle at this temperature. We had three axes and would chop down trees no wider than the mouth of a bowl. Anything bigger would be impossible to carry back.

Sweat prickled and we flung our hats off. They lay on the snow, six severed heads.

147

The fallen trees drew a tangled picture on the white ground, each branch leaving its own scar, a form of struggle. They took every opportunity to split open our fingers. The blood barely had a chance to flow before it froze over. Touching our wounds with our tongues, we tasted only a mild salty flavor. I've always felt that red is salty, yellow is bitter, and brown the undefinable taste of herbal medicine.

The ax blades dulled and seemed to grow heavier. I tried my best to lift mine higher, but it felt like it was passing through a part of my body each time it fell. It wasn't clear where—just a non-specific kind of pain.

At noon, because we had no food with us, we gobbled down handfuls of snow. The oxen were set loose, snuffling in the snow to find dried grass and the occasional yellowed leaf.

*

We still didn't have enough to fill the cart. Qiu'er suggested chopping down a big red pine—it would provide fuel for a week. If it wouldn't fit in the cart, we could drag it behind us. We used the two sharper axes to chop in alternate strokes, saving the third ax to clear the fallen branches. The first blow split the pine tree's fragrant bark and shook free its crown of accumulated snow. Tiny dots of cold burrowed into my neck, like needle pricks.

Shower after shower of wood chips went flying. One smacked Qiu'er in the face. No one saw this as a portent.

When we were halfway through the trunk, we heard a creaking noise. Inexperienced, we didn't know which direction it would fall in. The sound was coming from the gash in the trunk. The six of us pushed at it together, but it stayed firm. The wind blew through its branches. And still it didn't fall.

While the rest of us moved away, one person stayed behind to continue chopping. It didn't occur to anyone to move the oxen further off.

The tree remained vertical, trembling a tiny amount, reluctant to give way. Finally, very slowly, it picked a direction and descended with a roar, like a martyr reaching up to the blue sky.

The yellow bull had its head lowered, chewing at the dry grass. Who could have known the crown of branches would be so wide-reaching as to sweep it up too? Blood oozed from its head. We ran over and saw one of its eyes had fallen out onto the snow.

Its death was so sudden. To one side was a fresh pile of dung.

We didn't bring the great red pine back with us, just filled the cart with chopped wood. Then the six of us undid the harness and dragged the yellow bull back with us. Its carcass quickly froze solid, not leaving a single trace of blood on the snowy ground we passed over.

BURDEN

Back then, there was a cartoon—or more accurately a black-and-white propaganda image—depicting a granary rising higher than the clouds and a farm worker with a white kerchief over his head carrying a full sack, chest out, hand on hip, smiling atop a Z-shaped ramp.

I first saw this picture during the wheat harvest. In fact, it was while working late, carrying sack after sack of grain, that I tripped over the empty sacks at my feet, falling spread-eagled, my 160-jin burden landing on my head, shoving my nose into the ground, my lips and teeth slamming into the earth, filling my mouth with dirt and rendering my face colorful as a dye factory, leaving me stuck in the dormitory recuperating—around that time.

The cartoon was exquisitely drawn. Such a tall granary, the peasant so willing to hoist sacks weighing a couple of hundred jin up that ramp, a dozen or so stories, up to the rooftop where he'd pour his grain in, even turning his head a moment before that, as he broke through the cloud cover, to beam at us.

If he could have seen me—a pathetic creature who'd only ever climbed a three-story ramp, who'd only carried the standard 160-jin sacks, whose legs began to tremble after a mere dozen hours of labor—that warm smile might have turned cold: Damn your lack of fervor in the harvest.

I didn't pull aside the bandages that covered my nose and mouth to say anything to him.

Romanticism—I knew what this was, even before I'd heard of Shelley or Beethoven. I was happy to carry a sack full of revolutionary romanticism, to walk up the hundred-storey ramp of revolutionary romanticism, and of course, the greatest joy of all was to appear as the symbol of this revolutionary romanticism.

I cut out the picture and stuck it on the wall, where it served as a vivid contrast with my own face, myself being full of naturalistic realism.

When I was transferred to the propaganda unit in 1971, the hardest thing wasn't getting up early every morning to do sit-ups and headstands, shouting out slogans all the while, nor was it the long nights of organizing events. It was lifting sacks. The propaganda team weren't considered specialists, so we were expected to do other work when unoccupied, which basically meant carrying sacks. Normally, we'd have to supply the flour mill with raw material, and at harvest time we'd send the wheat to the warehouse. Truck after truck would arrive to be loaded—on the longest day, we worked from three in the morning to eight at night. Thinking about it now, I don't know how on earth I did all that, unless it was through divine intervention.

Anyone who did this job had a piece of white cloth, two and a half feet square, which we called a "shawl." It was draped over our heads and shoulders as we worked, keeping dirt off and preventing the sacks from rubbing our necks raw.

With the shawl in place, each sack had to be hoisted off the ground, a two- or three-person job. As soon as it was in the air, the carrier, poised in a lunge, would nimbly slide beneath it, using the momentum of the lift to come to a standing position, rolling his shoulders into place to tame the burden before starting to walk. This all had to happen very quickly, and with good teamwork. If the transfer to the shoulder went too slowly, the carrier wouldn't be able to stand.

Even more technique was required to pour the grain into the silo. Those who got it wrong ended up flinging their entire load in, then had to jump in to manually empty their sack, an exhausting task. Those in the know reached the top of the ramp, held their cargo by a corner, then vigorously shrugged it off their shoulders so the contents poured into the granary, leaving them swaggering back the way they came with an empty sack.

Yesterday, while flipping through an old journal, I found an entry written during one of these late nights:

October 11, 1973—day and night shift

On night duty. Writing this during a break. I'm shattered. My eyes are blurry. We worked through the day without a rest, even more exhausting than physical labor. And the night shift is awful too—beneath the lamp, my shadow is enormous, terrifying. The sack looks so natural pressed against my body. I can hardly believe it's me. I came to the border region four years ago, aged sixteen and a half. I've been carrying sacks more than two years.

Such a long time. I don't know what Ma would think if she could see me now.

To think I could write so mawkishly at such a time—petite bourgeois to my bones. How could you reform that?

Not every educated youth had to bear these burdens; most only had to help out at harvest time. It was different for those at the processing plants. The flour mills needed wheat from the silos every day, and the people assigned to these work units became known for their burden-bearing abilities.

The most magnificent instance I witnessed was in such a processing plant in 1974. It was harvest time, and there was a push to send the proletariat officer cadets to college. All of us longed to go back to the city and start studying again, but no one knew who ought to be sent. That day, the people who believed they should be chosen worked much harder than usual, lifting and carrying with great energy and silence. Jianjun, an educated youth from Beijing, was normally so lazy he knew he stood no chance now, so he came up with a weird idea—he ripped open the bottom of a sack and sewed it to the mouth of another, filling this giant thing with four hundred jin of wheat. If anyone could lift this and walk around the field once, surely they'd get everyone's vote.

This notion simplified all our complex guesswork, horse-trading, and argument. As a test of our abilities, nothing could be fairer or more straightforward. Four hundred jin of wheat tightly packed in one container. The first one to try was Lion Snout, who asked to personally select the five people who'd lift the sack onto his shoulders. The five he chose were all his good friends. At a shouted signal, they hoisted the burden, and he slipped underneath and stood tall. His legs wobbled, and while he stayed upright quite a while, he wasn't able to take a single step, and finally flung down the sack. He said, Not a damn one of you will be able to do this, if you don't believe me, try for yourself. The sack was packed anew, but for a while, nobody dared to step forward. Jianjun said if no one could do this, we could all forget about going to college. Sink, and we'd all sink together.

Old Sun wanted to go to college. He was tall and very thin, and his father was the head of the Design Academy. He normally never said anything. When he wanted to give it a go, everyone thought that was too cruel and told him to forget it, he might never be able to walk again. But he insisted, so we let him. The same five people helped to hoist, lifting the sack just as high as before. He got into position and shouldered the burden, standing upright, and mustering all his strength, managed to take a step, then another, eyes fixed to the ground. His skinny body was narrower than the sack. He sweated, face crimson. When he got halfway round, everyone started shouting in time with his footsteps. He was going to make it. At the end point, he didn't even have the energy to drop the sack, but just stood there, on the verge of collapse. We rushed over to relieve him of his burden. For a long time after that, his legs wouldn't stop shaking.

He didn't manage to leave in the end, even though we all voted for him. The higher-ups said laying bets and soliciting votes were worrying behavior, and decided instead to send someone who was unable to work.

After the college exams were reinstated, Old Sun won a place, became a research scholar, and finally left the country to be an academic. Now I think about it, someone who could lift a 400-jin sack of wheat wasn't going to be deterred by a couple of setbacks.

FIDDLE

There's a craft to playing the violin. To get from one note to another, you lift one finger and put down another. If you don't want the note to sound stupid, you have to make that finger tremble to produce a pleasing chant or warble. The technical word for this is "vibrato."

When you walked out from amongst the assembled troops into the gusting snow, violin case in hand, the term "educated youth" was still fresh and unfamiliar. This group hadn't just brought their luggage, their padded shoes and leather hats, they also had music with them. At night in front of the fire, a scratchy few notes on the violin was enough to silence everyone. This quietening down was very important, we needed entertainment.

There are also harmonics, produced by touching a finger to the string but not pressing down. These sound very sincere, very distant. Music made out of music, or else a sort of theoretical sound: we have to follow the rules to get it.

*

There was nowhere in the dormitory to store my violin. The bunks were already so crowded, trying to stick a musical instrument in there would be asking for trouble—the case would jostle people awake at night. The space underneath was already full of washbasins and dirty shoes, so that wouldn't work either. Violins aren't regular objects like lunchboxes or towels. They mostly lie there untouched, getting in the way.

Violin music didn't have a place here either. For instance, a group had just returned, black all over after loading three carriages with coal. You had to fetch water, wash your face, scrub yourself clean. If you dragged your exhausted carcass to one corner and practiced Kayser's *Etude Number 5* on your violin, you'd find it hard to make the music clear and elegant, amid the stink of sweat and those bare, scrawny torsos. The room was full of arms and bellies, water splashing resonantly as it washed those bodies. Curses and arguments rose and fell around the room. Now and then a smelly sock, dried hard, would fly past. Trying to concentrate on the bowing and fingering marked on the score, you'd do your best to get the pitch right, only to have someone, desperate for sleep, cry out, "Stop strangling that fucking chicken, kill me instead."

In fact, many people referred to playing the violin as "chicken slaughter." Please forgive the coarseness of those living amid cruelty. Understandable that they'd scream and shout rather than subject themselves to a Grade Two exercise. But you'd keep playing, and eventually they'd get used to it.

Violin strings go G D A E. You tune the A first, then the rest by playing chords: D and A, A and E, G and D. When both strings are in tune, the tones they produce fit together intimately, in harmony. No human voice could ever make such a sound.

When someone called it a "fiddle," you corrected him. He didn't care, he wanted to give this object a different name, the freshness demonstrating his innocence. He said, "This fiddle's not bad at all— touch it and it makes a noise." You had to admit that was an interesting way to put it, and it's true that not everything could be described in this way. A bed and its covers don't produce any sounds, but with a violin—touch it and it makes a noise.

And you have to confess that these words affected your steadfast practice of Kayser. When someone calls music "noise," that shakes the meaning of the word.

Your index finger plays a C, then an E on the same string. Shifting fingering in this way allows one hand to agilely produce every note on all four strings. There are rules to this, the positions are fixed and you can't shift them willy-nilly. You have to know exactly where every note sits, otherwise your playing goes out of tune.

He heard you practice from outside the window, and finally gave his opinion: you were just playing wretched little tunes better suited to bourgeois drinking houses. Couldn't your "Western erhu" produce something a peasant has actually heard of? For instance, *Mountain Climbing* or *Erlang Hill*. Let's hear these familiar tunes. What? A score? What do you want with a score? In my hometown, Tunxi, the blind fiddle player went all his life without seeing a score, and he knew all kinds of tunes, *Spying on the Lovers*, *The Little Widow* . . . Of course, these are all feudalist and capitalist and revisionist! Hey, why don't you play *Taking Tiger Mountain*?

When Paganini played at his fastest, many people said he must have had demonic assistance, and some in the audience even claimed to have seen the devil himself behind the musician on stage. Why demons and not angels? This question would make many violinists' pale faces go even paler! You have all these notes in your heart, because music can be something you hide away and never dare to retrieve.

In the end, the violin went into a little toolshed full of pickaxes, shovels, crowbars, ropes, gumboots. You and the instrument both breathed a sigh of relief.

Come the spring, when you went to visit the violin, a family of mice had made their home in its case. The velvet lining had been ripped to shreds and turned into a nest. They'd sharpened their teeth on the strings, and tunneled their way through the sides. The belly of the instrument now held a mound of wheat and corn. Everything had changed. There was no more music, and when you touched the violin, it no longer made a noise.

LABOR IN THREE ACTS

1. Weeds

The longest stretch of land is eighteen kilometers, so far you can't see the edge.

You don't know how many times you've had to raise your hoe along those eighteen kilometers, sun overhead, steam rising off the land.

These shoots are unknowable, swaying away, looking even tinier as you labor above them. Green shoots, green grass. Does it hurt the turf to be uprooted, broken stems seeping damply?

You thrust the hoe out as far as possible, then haul it back, again and again, left and right. Dirt flies up your trousers, all the way to your collar, where it mingles with sweat. Fresh, rain-washed soil, soaking up perspiration, filthy and intimate. Rain spatters sturdily over the fields. Your clothes are wet, your chest is wet, and your bones too.

Your teeth chatter. The wind surges toward you, rain slants into your eyes. Nowhere to hide. Unless someone has the power to force out the sun's dome.

Fallen grass springs up with the rain, and half a day's labor vanishes.

In the pocket of your shirt, a scrap of paper, too sodden to unfold. You can't think what it is, and fumble opening it. A corner, a section.

You can decipher a couple of lines.

Come or don't come . . .

Only . . . cares

No idea what these words mean. Nothing to do with you, not even the handwriting. What's it doing in your pocket? You can't imagine. Spread it out on a dirt mound. When it's dry, see if you can open it up and find out more.

The hoe is wet and heavy. Never a good day for work, neither in the sun nor rain. Head down, hoeing, shoots grass shoots grass shoots grass. The same green. The difference is a judgement call. A man-made difference. Imagine ten thousand mu covered in shoots, like a public square, a book printed with just one word so that's all you see as you flip the pages.

Lunch arrives.

You see the river bend ahead, the end of dry land. Water-fowl with hatchlings. When they rise into the sky, their cries sound different than usual.

Goshawks even higher up.

You've never crossed over to the marsh there, that's not your territory. Not farmland but nature, a pocket your hands will never reach into.

Your clothes dry.

You smell the river. New blisters on your hand. Pain. A little longer, almost there.

The swampland has tiger lilies and white lilies, who watch as the workers hoe their way over. Such beauty makes a hard-working, coarse laborer feel vulgar.

Wash your hands in the river and turn back. In the evening, moles poke their heads above ground, tramping heavily over dead grass.

Dusk rushes in from all directions.

The scrap of paper has dried. Now you can see it starts with your name. It's a note, a love letter to you.

The words at the end are washed away. Her name is gone. She

wrote this message and slipped it into your pocket, then abruptly vanished. No trace.

You can't think who this might be. There are more than two hundred women in this division. You can't recall all their names. If only you knew who she was.

Read out loud the lines that remain. Weeds listen in the wind, the hoed and broken grass.

2. Wheat

In July 1994, I travel to Tongjiang from Shuangyashan. The wheat is yellow but not ready to be harvested yet, wheat all along the way, which I can see more clearly when the vehicle stops.

The wheat hasn't changed much in twenty years. Crops don't age. If you allow them to remain in the soil, what you witness is not birth and death, but year after year, a grain of wheat coming back to its beginning. They always return to their original state, growing for the sake of the next generation's youth. We can't do this, us humans. I've hoped for an end to it all, but that's not attainable.

Two decades ago, when I walked into a field of wheat, I thought only of how to cut it down and carry it away. Now for all I know, my thinking is more like the wheat itself—I hope it can stay there longer. Or else place a seed into the soil, and after winter, watch an identical stalk of wheat emerge in the same place—making you feel that no time has passed.

The wheat stalk's bristles jab at you, its jagged edges sharp as a saw. Snap one in two, blow away the chaff, leaving a few grains behind. They gleam in your palm, solemn as gemstones.

Place the grains in your mouth as the vast swathe of wheat sways before you. You chew hard, and the bristles catch at your clothes, scarring your skin. You chew, swallowing their cries.

If it gets to autumn and no one comes for the wheat, does it feel lonely? You've seen wheat in the rain, standing amid falling water, grains scattering, leaving the stalks weightless, like an insect's empty carapace. Hold them in your hand, and nothing comes out. At that point, all you can do is set them on fire, so the ashes fertilize the soil.

Amid the flames, field mice scamper. If they can't escape, they die there. A burned field is much purer than a harvested one. Before winter comes, it contains only soil, nothing else.

Time to go. The driver is smoking by the roadside. He feels differently than I do when he looks at the wheat (reminding me of someone from twenty years ago). His expression would once have been familiar to me.

3. Horse

The horse, churning words around his mouth, knows a fair amount. The way a horse looks at another horse is how we appear when we're being kind.

A horse's exhaustion is more noble than mine. He doesn't speak of tiredness and asks for nothing, wary of attracting pity. He works on, beautifully.

Horses' hides, when they perspire, smell strongly of themselves.

One day in fall, I walk a dark horse down a slope, a dozen daisies braided through its mane. I don't own a mirror large enough for a horse, but if it likes it can see its reflection in the stream.

As I lead it along, I hear the evening bell signaling the end of the workday. Ahead of us the sun is setting, and when I look back into the horse's eyes, I see a red mountain range.

GREEN SHOOTS

Because the Great Northern Waste was free of frost so little of the year, most crops wouldn't thrive there. On the other hand, with the fertile soil and dramatic swings from hot to cold, anything that did survive would grow to be extraordinarily plump and flavorful. During the long winter (six months), our staple food (white noodles) remained the same, and the side dishes seldom varied: potatoes and cabbages, turned into soup or fried, fried or turned into soup. Through the entire season, the canteen menu scrawled on the chalkboard hardly ever needed to be altered. Of course, the ingredients occasionally changed. For instance, if a cow died, the vegetables would be served with beef. If a pig died, as long as it didn't have swine pox, there'd be pork rind or fatty meat. But these were rare occurrences, because pigs and cows didn't often die. Once, I ate some beef from a cow struck dead by lightning, but its flesh was tough and flavorless, meat only in name, its goodness zapped away by electricity. Like gnawing on wax. Old sows didn't taste good either, bland and chewy as rubber. Still, there was the reassuring sensation of tasting meat, however loosely defined. One time, I got to enjoy some delicious veal. After I'd eaten, my schoolmate Lion Snout told me it was a young female, killed when a bull tried to mount her. That made me feel the cruelty behind the flavor, as if I'd helped out a scoundrel. I cursed the blabbermouth. Why tell me something like that?

Potato and cabbage were so important that, as soon as autumn arrived, we'd send teams out to quickly harvest them. Cart after cart would get unloaded into the storage cellar, and after thousands of vegetables had gone through the narrow opening, our winter was secure. We could stay alive as long as these two things kept appearing on our tables. The only alternative were pickles known as "scare away guests." If it had come to that, we'd have ended up as shriveled as the radishes in the pickle vat.

Vegetable cellars were crucial in our lives, but at the time, most divisions didn't have a decent one, probably because of the belief that Revolution was more important than life, and that the harder your existence, the closer you were to the Revolution. After all these excellent potatoes and cabbages were harvested, if they weren't put away in time, the snow would arrive and they'd end up frozen solid, at which point, the only recipe left was: prize one free with a pickax, thaw it, boil it, serve it. Even the greatest imagination couldn't make these dishes taste anything but acrid. Neither the sweetness nor bitterness of life was discernible in them any longer.

As we went through the process of being rehabilitated, us educated youths became aware of the need for a vegetable cellar, accepting that eating unfrozen potatoes without beef might not be harmful to the Revolution. So we dug a deep, wide pit, hastily shoveling the vegetables in and putting a roof over them before the snow arrived. After that, you'd often see the duty cook climbing down into the cellar, emerging with basket after basket of warm potatoes or cabbages, a sight that made us feel life was good and under control.

These cellars had other uses, though we only discovered this after the incident. I went down into ours a few times, when I was called upon to assist the cooks. There was an electric light that, when turned on, illuminated the potatoes and cabbages' peaceful faces. There was no wind or snow down here, but it wasn't hot, and the air was heavy with sourness. Your hand had the power to choose, and all these vegetables, imprisoned so long, would glare at you coldly.

A person picking the next victim to be eaten cannot expect a warm welcome in a vegetable cellar. I couldn't feel good down there, no matter how much it added to our existence. It felt like a dungeon full of lives I'd never get to know.

Third Camp, Eighteenth Company was a small group, so naturally their cellar was small and cozy too. At the time, dalliances between educated youths rarely progressed beyond a spiritual level, partly because love was forbidden, but even more because we had no opportunity to so much as talk. Every division had hundreds of eyes looking out for this sort of thing—imagine being romantic under such scrutiny! Courage wasn't enough. And so most relationships took place under conditions of great secrecy, like working undercover, carried out through facial expressions and code words, or even more often, when forcibly separated, by thought alone. Love like this carried the intensity of suffering, so every second together was worth a thousand pieces of gold. Most people found themselves like bows stretched to breaking point.

Love stimulates ingenuity. One couple came up with the idea of using the cellar. The boy was a Tianjin educated youth, our company platoon leader, normally dignified and severe. The girl was from Tianjin too, placid and soft-spoken, ordinary looking. Before this happened, no one had any idea they were together (up till then, I'd thought it would take superhuman ability to conceal love, but the Cultural Revolution produced just such superhumans). I don't know how often they met there—when I get to this part, I think of Juliet's tomb.

We found their naked bodies in the cellar. The girl was a little closer to the entrance, as if she'd struggled to get out. The boy probably died faster, gloriously, no suffering on his face. They looked like stage props or perhaps sculptures, sprawled separately (but possibly connected), their souls scattered among those silent winter vegetables.

We dragged their corpses from the warm cellar. I don't know why none of us thought of putting clothes on them, but their pale bodies flopped naked on the snow, not moving, black manes spreading over the white ground, only the tiny hairs on their bodies stirring in the wind—signal flags sending a final message.

They shouldn't have lit a coal-burning stove in an enclosed space.

Even after all these years, I often recall this incident and find myself imagining the loving scenes I didn't actually witness. I don't know why this is. Perhaps deaths like these, beautiful as art, shouldn't cause regret or sadness. Which of us is fit to feel pity?

The entire company refused to eat the stored vegetables, perhaps afraid of stirring something up. In fact, they wouldn't go near the cellar at all, so it fell into disuse and caved in. That spring, the buried potatoes sprouted, sending shoots up through the soil, a patch of bright green.

HEART-TO-HEART

I was hauling sacks of wheat when it started to rain, so I dashed
into the granary to get my gumboots. Inside, two soldiers whose
conduct was usually excellent were sitting knee-to-knee, having a
heart-to-heart. A man and a woman. This was a startling scene to
be faced with after running in from the rain and from my work,
but I was the one who felt embarrassed. They'd been discussing
the weighty issue: six decades of putting down roots in the bor-
derlands. To think I'd interrupted them over something as trivial
as a pair of gumboots! While I looked for my boots, they stayed
silent—what they had to say was too important to be overheard by
someone searching for footwear. Besides, our brothers the farmers
had no gumboots, and didn't they do their work just the same? We
were snatching food from the mouth of the dragon, and each sack
of wheat we hauled was an achievement on behalf of the People.
How much time was I going to waste, running around trying to
find my gumboots?

In the end, I went back to work without my gumboots. Laboring
away in the rain, everyone looked very tragic, lines of water trick-
ling down their faces, like sweat but not, like tears but not. Rain
pouring in curtains over them. Wheat hung over our shoulders, *our*
wheat—we'd planted it in the summer, and now we were taking it

back. We were all running, whether on level ground or up the ramp, laden down or empty handed.

Even those who were unable to run made faces that looked as if they were running.

Cart after cart was emptied and rolled away, while the rain continued, and so did the heart-to-heart. Those two people had transcended labor. What were they talking about? Could they find a subject in the mud caked around my legs? Then again, if you asked me to talk about the mud, I'd rather start with the gumboots.

I needed a drink of water. Sure, it was raining, but that didn't mean us workers could go without water. The wheat no longer needed watering, but its owners did, even in this storm. When I called out that I was thirsty, many others said they were too. We covered the wheat with a tarpaulin and squatted down, waiting for an imaginary person to boil water and bring it to us.

I'm not one for heart-to-hearts. I believe people who seek out others for conversation don't only tell the truth but also shove in a big pile of lies. Which is not to say I don't lie or am unwilling to lie, but I'm reluctant to do so under the rubric of a heart-to-heart.

What an enchanting phrase, "heart-to-heart." And how lucky we are, to have so many people we can talk to in this world. A little like Xiang Lin's wife from the Lu Xun short story?

One evening, a girl came over while I was doing laundry. She didn't say she wanted a heart-to-heart, but I knew she'd been after a good chat for some time. The clothes I was washing were filthy, and the colors were running. I knew it was pointless doing laundry in a tub of filthy water, so I hoped whatever she had to say could help dispel my frustration.

She began with idle chatter, pacing back and forth, picking up this and that, bumping into the gong (used to summon us to emergency meetings), slipping a hand into her shoe right in front of me to pull up her sock. When she was ready to speak she sat down, only to stand up again when she couldn't get the words out.

Finally, she managed half a sentence: ". . . you ought to draw a clear line between your family . . ." and with that she was gone, pulling the door shut behind her.

I must admit I hadn't been expecting that; it certainly wasn't how I'd imagined our heart-to-heart. I felt she ought to have done this instead:

She pushes open the door, takes off her scarf and comes over to help me with the laundry. As we chat, she tells me to fetch some clean water. Emptying out my pockets, she finds bits of paper, falling apart from their soaking. To a soundtrack of lathering and wringing, she asks, "Have you had a letter from home?" When I answer yes, she asks, "What did it say?" I tell her and she turns back to the laundry, saying simply, "You ought to draw a clear line between your family and yourself."

If she'd done that, perhaps I'd have been moved to tears. And maybe when the laundry was done, I'd have invited her out for a moonlit walk, and a deeper conversation.

This was no heart-to-heart, but a spleen-to-spleen, or maybe a gall-to-gall. I knew this wasn't what she'd wanted to say that evening. Perhaps it was more like, "You're quite adorable, and I like you." (Later, I would have confirmation of this.) Yet for some reason, she'd gone on about "a clear line." (Maybe she'd reached for these words out of force of habit, or maybe she'd gone from heart-to-heart to foot-in-mouth.)

Finally, I rebelled against heart-to-hearts. Seeing others murmuring sweet nothings in the name of Revolution, sitting knee-to-knee, one-on-one, comrade-to-comrade. I didn't feel lonely. I'd rather be summoned by the authorities for a chat. At least that way I'd be prepared, and it wouldn't come as a shock.

So that day as we worked in the rain, when I saw the couple having their heart-to-heart, I didn't feel envy or anger. I really was thirsty when I said I needed a drink, I wasn't throwing a tantrum, and didn't mean to make everyone stop work. Yet when we had our meeting that evening, one person from the couple who'd enjoyed a heart-to-heart all day denounced me viciously, saying I didn't like hard work and had induced everyone to laze around. Confused, I could only stammer that it hadn't been like that. After that, I don't know why I talked and talked, until finally I took the teacup in my hand and smashed it into that man's face. I really couldn't tell you what I was feeling at the time. Honestly, I'm not good with words.

THE FORGED LOVE LETTER

The false words I've written in this life include a love letter.

In the Great Northern Waste, we spent half the days of the year staring into whiteness. The purity and monotony of snow soon gave rise to boredom. The best way to make time pass was gambling; the second was practical jokes.

Bottle Cap was one of my schoolmates; we could no longer remember the origin of his nickname. He was a year or two older than the rest of us, and universally loathed for his grubbiness, laziness, and gluttony. His body was home to an abundance of vermin: lice were the most numerous (infantry), then bedbugs (tank regiments) and finally fleas (the air force). Supporting so many parasites left him always looking pale. All day long he sat there, hands burrowing beneath his clothes to inspect and redeploy his forces. From time to time, he mumbled to himself. Most of Bottle Cap's energy went on dealing with these bugs, filling his life with loneliness and depression.

Forging a love letter to send him was the brainwave of another schoolmate, Roast Chicken. We had a vague notion that it would lift him out of his despair. Once the idea was hatched, the task of writing fell to me. Back then, I hadn't yet come across books like *The Compendium of Love Letters* or *The Collected Poems of Xi Murong*, so I was creating words from thin air. To make it more lively, I threw in some proverbs and colloquialisms. I can still remember one or two lines: "XXX, you're quite a cute little fellow! Like they say, to water a flower you water the roots, to touch a person you touch her heart . . . If you'd like to get to know me, see me, love me, let's meet outside the Supply and Marketing Co-op, noon on such-and-such date." The sign-off was a popular one at the time, "You know who." I sprinkled exclamation marks liberally through the text, and Roast Chicken approved when he'd read it over. To show his admiration for my literary skills, he bought me a bottle of low-quality seed wine (I guess that was the first payment I ever received for my writing).

We placed the love letter on Bottle Cap's filthy, messy bunk. Then we sat nearby, playing cards and keeping an eye on his every movement. He went through roughly the following sequence of events: enter room, climb onto upper bunk, discover love letter, express shock, sit down to read it through, lie down to read it again, stare into space and read it one more time, put letter away. Light was emanating from his face.

Over the next few days, Bottle Cap boiled huge quantities of water to disinfect his bedding and clothes. The colors bled, leaving our sleeping area draped with trousers and jackets in suspicious shades, hanging up to dry. In the meantime, he managed to borrow a woolen coat, a pair of slip-on shoes, and leather gloves.

Everyone could see he was in a frenzy preparing for this false date. Before long, more than three hundred educated youths knew what was going on, while he alone remained in ignorance. This seemed rather cruel; I dropped a couple of hints, but it was no use, he was simply too excited. The story had to be played to its end.

It was a stirring sight: Bottle Cap standing beneath a snowy sky, clad in thin and ill-fitting clothes, waiting in front of the Co-op. The entire cohort of educated youths stood pressed against the dormitory's rear windows, watching him. Snowflakes alighted on his head, his eyelashes, his body, snow on top of snow. Bottle Cap stood patiently and steadfastly, waiting for his moment. He couldn't even spare time to brush the snow off his hair. The pure snow dyed him white. He stood his ground, preparing to become a statue.

Shame blossomed in our hearts. Bottle Cap's frank determination made us feel guilty.

Roast Chicken flung open the window and shouted to him. Everyone shouted to him.

Finally, a couple of people leaped from their window and bundled him indoors, very much against his will.

For a few days afterward, he didn't say a word as he slunk in and out of the dorm, still dressed in his date outfit. We were a little worried about him, and one night I pulled out my seed wine and offered to share it with him. Halfway through the bottle, he said he didn't hate us because of what had happened, and in fact didn't believe the letter had been forged. He was certain a girl *had* written just such a passionate letter to him, but we'd shown up too early and scared her off. One day, she'd arrange another meeting with him.

There was nothing more to be said. He lived with such purpose, such hope. How foolish the rest of us seemed at that moment.

REMEMBERING CERTAIN PEOPLE

Accidents happened all the time in the Great Northern Waste. One frosty winter, some people were loading coal at the train station. An icy layer had formed over the coal heap, but they found a soft spot and dug in, getting deeper and deeper. Eventually the frozen outer shell had nothing to support it and collapsed, crushing two educated youths from Beijing, both girls. I didn't feel very much when I heard about this. When I think of it now, though, I realize they were just seventeen or eighteen. They'd never loved, never truly lived! As I write this, I wonder who still remembers them. It's been more than a decade. (That was true at the time I wrote those words, but it's now actually been four decades.) If souls exist, I hope theirs can read what I'm writing.

Accidents happened frequently at the quarry, where the work involved loose shale and explosives, not to mention sledgehammers and drill rods, which could hurt a lot if you so much as touched them. The quarry guys were all pretty sturdy—they had to be, wielding those huge hammers every day—while the girls handled the rods. We envied them—it must have been nice that men and women could be together there, even if they didn't get to speak. I saw them setting explosives, filling a cave with bundle after bundle of them, then setting them off. It took guts to be the person in charge of the fuses: you had to light more than a dozen, one by one, and they'd go off as soon as you reached shelter. Educated youths never minded this sort of work. The cigarettes they used were government-provided, so they'd compete to see who could light the most fuses from a single one, keeping the remaining packets to smoke themselves.

This time it was the blast that went wrong. Half an hour after the fuses were lit, they still hadn't gone off. When getting rid of a defective bomb, the deputy instructor and platoon leader were supposed to take charge together. An educated youth from Beijing had done something wrong and wanted to get out of the doghouse, so he came too. When they were almost at the mouth of the cave, there was an explosion. The deputy instructor and platoon leader vanished in an instant. The educated youth hadn't yet rounded the corner and was sheltered by a large rock. The force of the blast threw him some distance, and he couldn't stop shouting, "Mother-fucker, motherfucker!"

Down from the quarry was a river, and on the opposite shore we found scattered hands, bones and toes. It wasn't clear who each body part belonged to. All we knew was two educated youths were dead, one from Shanghai and one from Tianjin. Back then, we didn't fear death, or at least it wasn't a sensitive matter. No one spent much time thinking about death—if I die, I die! We had no time for more thought. I only met one person back then who seemed truly grief-stricken in the presence of death: Liang Ming's father.

Wanhua Brigade consisted of just three buildings, and back when it was Wanfa Village, only thirty-odd households lived here. It became Wanhua after the brigade was stationed here. Three desolate rows of houses on the way from First Camp to the Regimental Headquarters. There were piles of barley straw in front of these buildings, and when you drove up, you'd always see female educated youths peeing here. They'd been there over a month but there were still no toilets in Wanhua Brigade, not even an outhouse. The girls had no choice but to piss behind these straw heaps, facing away from the buildings but toward the main road.

The Great Northern Waste was full of flies. Sometimes you'd see a black steamed bun in the drawer—a layer of flies covering its entire surface. Swat them away to make it turn white again. It was common to find yourself ingesting a fly while drinking your soup or eating your meal.

How precious the educated youths were, when they first arrived! But dysentery often struck. Liang Ming was not yet seventeen. Her father was a diplomatic officer stationed overseas; her mother was a teacher. She was the sort of girl you used to see in the sixties: beautiful, innocent, eyes full of sunshine. While she was at Wanhua, she contracted dysentery and was dead in less than a day. This was just over a month after we were sent down. Our classmate had been fine, then a day later she was dead and buried on a distant hillside. We were so young, once we got over the fright, we stopped thinking about it. We continued pissing behind the barley straw and eating flyblown steamed buns.

Winter passed and spring arrived. A man in a woolen coat showed up in Wanhua on a rickety large-wheeled tractor covered in mud. Only when he entered the dormitory did we find out he was Liang Ming's dad. He gave us all cigarettes (Chunghwa, an expensive brand). Looking at all the youngsters in front of him, he didn't show his sadness. He went by himself to Liang Ming's bunk and touched her things, not saying a word, then went for a stroll around the brigade.

When he came back, he asked the brigade commander if he could borrow a broom before having a look at Liang Ming's grave. The commander was Liu the File, a very short, sturdy guy. He found a brand-new broom and sent the father off on a tractor to the eastern hills. Several Beijing educated youths went along with him. The vehicle stopped by the grave and all of a sudden I felt lonely and cold. Liang Ming was just lying there, all alone every single day. Such a wonderful girl, why did she have to die? There was nothing around—to the south were sloping grasslands, and the grave was like a lifeless eye.

Liang Ming's dad got off the tractor with his broom, and when he got closer, he took off his hat. "Ming, Daddy's here," he said. "It's taken me so long to come." Finally, he cried. We stood behind him, also sobbing. I could sense there was a lot he wanted to say, but no more words came out, he just cried as he swept the grave, like combing his daughter's hair. After all these years, I still remember those two sentences spoken in his southern accent.

The next day, the regimental commander arrived at Wanhua in a jeep. Only now did we learn that Liang Ming's father had flown from France to Beijing, and without even going home, caught the next flight to Harbin, then made his way to our brigade. He hadn't told anyone, just hitched a ride on a broken-down old tractor. (When I had a daughter of my own, I would learn for myself how much strength those emotions can bring you.) The commander rushed over when he heard the news, first to apologize, then to ask if the father had any requests. (I don't understand why this question was asked. What kind of request could bring back his daughter?) Liang Ming's dad was silent for quite a while, then finally he said, "Build a toilet for the girls."

As Liang Ming's dad was leaving, he hugged each of us goodbye and we all wept. Maybe we were affected by his sorrow, or thinking of our own families.

Later, the best toilet in the whole brigade was constructed in Wanhua, made of huge slabs of stone weighing 360 jin each.

The next time I passed through Wanhua, I saw the new building: an eye-catching grayish-white toilet.

COMPOSITION

The day I'd decided to compose a tune, I waited for it to get dark, and hoped for a blackout—I had candles at the ready.

I'd borrowed a room (an office). I'd heard the heating went off at night, and it got so cold that any water left in the teacups would freeze. I didn't care. By cold candlelight, I hummed and wrote my song. Even unborn, it already seemed to have an undimmable brilliance.

No one had told me to write a tune, I wanted to do it myself. Yet no song issued naturally from my mouth. To be more accurate, I wanted to create a song. I would perform it in Jiamusi, sung by me alone, a solo. I would sing a song I'd written myself. An exciting thought.

The sky darkened. Stars gleamed like nails. If only they were words or notes . . .

A song needs lyrics. I'd write the words first, then add the tune on subsequent nights.

I started work and realized I didn't have much going for me apart from enthusiasm. I didn't even know what the song would be about. I'd thought a subject would come to me with the cold and candlelight, but that wasn't how it worked. The flames grew longer and the candles shorter, and the cold penetrated my heart. Nothing arrived, not a single word. I kept asking myself, You wanted to write a song, didn't you? So write! Write!

I started yearning for dawn, I needed sleep, it was too cold, I wished I were back in the dorm. I hadn't written a single word, no one could ever find out how this had turned out, I ought to ignore everyone when I headed back after dawn, acting as though I were completely absorbed by the act of composition.

The next day, no one asked me what I'd got up to the night before. They had things on their mind too, but not songs. The cause of my unhappiness felt self-indulgent.

I returned to the room with my pen and paper. My hand shook as I lit the candles. Would the same thing happen again? I got a sense of my surroundings, and five words came to mind: cold light burnishes her armor. A lyric from *The Ballad of Mulan*, which I'd learnt in fifth grade. I wrote it down, feeling I'd accomplished something—there were words on the page, and sure they didn't belong to me, but perhaps I could change them . . .

I decided to write a song about horseback patrol, though I'd never been on a horse, nor on patrol. Still that was the song I would write, partly inspired by the words, "cold light burnishes her armor."

I wrote about horses, rifles, the Fatherland behind me, thousands of blazing hearth fires, facing imperialist Soviet invaders. I expressed the duty and loneliness of the rider. All night long, I sat in a wooden chair, imagination galloping ahead. By dawn I had two verses and a chorus, very standard. I wasn't sleepy at all. Immersed in the act of creation, I was already thinking about the tune.

I emerged from the hut with several melodies swirling around my mind, and unable to stop myself, I began singing beneath the starry sky.

The next day, everyone in the brigade was talking about someone who'd apparently suffered an outbreak of hysteria the night before, running around bare-assed and warbling in the snow, sleepwalking, accidentally frightening away a wolf who'd come hunting pigs. Finally awakened by the cold, he ran back inside. I knew they were talking about me, but I didn't mind this slander. Nothing could diminish my dedication to songwriting.

I urgently asked Dawei, a good singer, about the relationship between major and minor keys. Having grasped the difference between do-mi-sol and re-fa-la, I had decided to create something solemn and lyrical in a major key.

I didn't expect a nap to put a dent in my creativity. That night, before getting to the same point as before, I dozed off in front of the candles, drooling onto my blank paper. I was awakened by someone arriving for work in the morning—not the person who lent me the office—who expressed shock and puzzlement that anyone would abandon a perfectly good bed to come drool in a freezing cold office by candlelight, all in the flimsy name of composition. He handed me my sheets of paper, a gesture filled with pity and contempt.

I had a fever; I'd caught a chill. Lying sick in bed, I dreamed of falling from a cliff. The medic said I needed an injection.

My body stank of sweat, discomfiting her. She had no idea I'd been too busy composing to bathe or do laundry. She reached into her aluminum case for a needle to stick in my flesh. Hearing her break the glass seal, the first note came to me: a chord played by trumpet, trombone, and tenor horn for two bars. Next the strings, wide open and placid, like the snowscape of the Great Northern Waste, unchanging for six months at a time. Finally, hoofbeats, faint then growing louder. To this beat, the singer would launch into a long note, followed by a section in 2/4 (how cold an alcohol-soaked cotton ball feels against a feverish buttock). Then an interlude, a slower beat, like the swaying shoulders of a Mongolian dance, a sort of savage energy (penicillin is the most painful; water-based shots hurt more than oil). More singing against this stable structure. Another long note, then hoofbeats again, leading to the second section (after the needle comes out, press down with a cotton ball). A resounding chorus, passing between F and G, effortlessly reaching for the high note, lingering eight beats on the A, finishing on the F. (Pulling trousers back up unashamed, a patient has no gender. I tighten my belt a notch—I've lost weight, all because of composition.) Probably end on a strong beat, because the song started on a weak one. Drag it out five counts, that should be enough.

When I wrote out the song, many people insisted I must have copied it from somewhere (I know that was a form of praise). Some said it was a pretty good effort for an educated youth.

During rehearsals, I talked about how I came up with the tune and the process of composition, but the musicians couldn't make it work. Now that it had been written out, it felt incomplete. Same with me—the feelings I had during my fever had completely disappeared. To be accurate, having written this song, I found it departing from me in the end.

MISFIRE

You were still at Eighteenth Brigade at the time. Just before I left, we caught a wild chicken in the snow. It had a broken wing and we kept it in a bamboo basket. Remember that? Feathers like satin, cool to the touch. We hugged it and tried to feed it steamed buns, but it refused, like a hero going on hunger strike. After I'd left, the rest of you ate the chicken. Such a beautiful bird, devoured by you. When I came back for my luggage, I saw a chunk of ice with brilliantly-colored chicken feathers frozen in it, suspended amidst filth, a vision of fallen splendor. I like images like this, whether of people or objects, that convey the reality of cruelty. Seeing a good thing ruined is forceful, carving it into your existence like a knife blade.

None of you were happy about me going. Only one person got chosen from the whole brigade, and it was me, a regular guy—no one would have expected me to get sent to the police brigade to fetch a gun. Not even me. Back then, ordinary people had more opportunities. I got on the Model-28 tractor that would take me away. Hardly anyone came to see me off, for which I was grateful. I could see the rest of you in the distance, making fertilizer granules at the threshing floor. Life hadn't changed for you, but it had for me. Feeling different made me think for a moment that I shouldn't be an ordinary person.

The gun was issued without much ceremony—just an old sub-machine gun. Now I think of it, this was a prop from this portion of my life. I held it up for the camera, striking a pose, a demonstration of status. The gun was more important than me. As soon as it appeared, one had to strike certain postures and speak certain lines. Nothing more enthralling for a "literary hero." Now you have a gun, you have a better chance than most people of becoming a hero, like a warrior in a Peking opera, never letting slip an opportunity to appear in public. The poems you read come from the barrel of a gun, with openings like, "Gun, revolutionary gun, gun of battle . . ."

Yet when it came to actually using this gun as a weapon, I got stage fright. I never thought the day would come when I'd have to step onto a real battlefield. All I wanted was to keep up the relationship of actor and prop, happily holding the unloaded rifle and performing in a play with no plot: night patrol, sentry duty.

. . . So did you hear about the misfire?

It wasn't that big a deal, but it was bad for me. Remember the grouch from Third Brigade, the local guy who played the banhu? Yes, him! He got caught in bed with an educated youth from Tianjin, and they sentenced him to labor reform. Tired, hungry work.

That day, I was on guard duty during their lunch break. They got a couple of steamed buns each, plus some "scare away guests" pickles. I never usually played with my gun, but for some reason I was fiddling with my rifle bolt when the weapon slipped out of my hand, and all seven bullets were discharged. The barrel had been pointing at the ground and I thought no one was hurt, but a moment later I noticed the grouch's heel was bleeding. In a panic, I ordered another convict to piggyback him to the medical center. The grouch stared at the bleeding as if he wasn't the one who'd been shot and kept chewing on his steamed bun—too hungry to feel pain. The other convict tried to lift him, but the grouch said, Hang on, let me finish eating this first.

With that, he turned back to the remaining bun, bleeding freely from his heel the whole time.

I was ready to collapse from fear. The way the grouch ate that steamed bun terrified me. I remembered as a kid, my classmates and I would fling stones at each other for fun. When one boy got hit in the head, he started sobbing and so did I. The grouch didn't cry, though, he just kept eating. Nothing could induce him to abandon his bun, not even if the sky collapsed. Like pissing, once you get going you couldn't stop. He went on gobbling down that bun.

To this day, I don't understand how someone could be so hungry as to not feel pain. The steamed bun was like his life—he clutched it so tight, you'd have thought it would vanish if he'd let it go. Perhaps in that moment he wasn't thinking about life or death, and his world contained nothing but that steamed bun. Right then, was it death or hunger that felt more real, more urgent, more significant?

The year I turned thirty-eight, I suddenly began to fear death, grabbing at this faraway thing and troubling myself with it daily, needlessly scaring myself till I could barely function. Then I remembered the grouch after the misfire and understood my fear of death was the act of a well-fed person trying to spice up his life. If you didn't become enlightened after experiencing something like that, what kind of life could possibly make you wise up?

Finally I'd realized I was at best an ordinary person, or perhaps a little less than ordinary. Some words had misled me, that's all. In fact, my goal in life was to be a regular guy, not to cause disaster, not to be a hero. Even if I worked hard, all I'd ever be was a performer, someone who relied on his props.

The grouch was left with a limp. The next time he went on stage to play the banhu, he looked rather pitiable. Meanwhile, I turned in my rifle and joined the pig-feeding squad.

I never tried to get in touch with him after I'd returned to Beijing. That was bad of me, but when I thought of him eating that steamed bun, I felt nothing I had to say could ever truly reach him.

WOMEN

Do you remember all the illicit foods we ate back then? I've never had such tasty fresh dog meat. A pinch of salt in the stew to bring out its true flavor. Such a scrawny dog, just like us.

Oh! Right, there was the time we ate the flesh of a white horse that got sick and died, lying there in the field like a giant toy, flies buzzing around its eyes. You hacked off one of its rear legs with an ax and schlepped it back, pretending to be a farmer carrying his plowshare. Not a bad impersonation, apart from the dripping blood that spattered the road behind us.

Those were bitter days, but we found the sweetness in them. When I look for sweetness in my life now, there is none. We were seventeen, just a bunch of kids, ten or twenty thousand of us dumped in the snowy plains. Planting grain in the spring, harvesting it in the fall, hiking into the woods on frosty days to get firewood. Such massive days. I can't forget the vastness of those days, they've etched themselves into my heart.

Remember getting wood from the hills? That's how Cricket was crushed to death. The trees were supposed to fall uphill, but a black birch bounced back in the other direction, and he couldn't get out of the way in time. The trunk landed on him.

Like the rest of you, he was from Yuyuantan High School. We buried him where he lay. If we looked for it now, we might not even be able to find the mound. That might be for the best, he's part of the hill now. Ha.

Well, what else can I do but laugh?

Women weren't allowed to fetch lumber from the hill, a long-standing local custom. Most of the people who went were unmarried "raw eggs" or old guys. The ones with families refused, not even for money. Nothing must disturb the beauty of a spring night—they understood that.

For more than thirty days, you wouldn't see a woman, not even a glimpse. Day after day, sawing away, carrying lumber. Kneeling in the snow, facing the hills, facing the trees. When you got bored, you'd turn your cry of "timber!" into a sort of song.

Not seeing women felt like being brought into a familiar room, but when you reached for the light pull, it wasn't there, no matter how much you groped—the cord had snapped, and the room would stay dark, a dark you couldn't do anything about, leaving you anxious and lonely.

As soon as night fell, you'd sit in our tent and regale us with *The Rise and Fall of the Third Reich*. Wind and snow filled the outside air, while we had a couple of kerosene lamps and a fire blazing away. You managed to make these political developments sound enthralling, and everyone rushed to offer you cigarettes and drinks. We pursued you night after night, clamoring to serve you. That was naughty of you.

We lumberjacks demanded booze before we'd so much as pick up a saw. We set off with half a jin of baijiu and gulped a mouthful for each tree we felled. No need to bring water, we scooped up snow from the ground and crunched it. Boozing was joyous back then, but nowadays the most I can manage is a little beer.

You'd counted wrong—it was actually the thirty-sixth day, by which time you'd switched to talking about *The Three Musketeers* and Walter Scott's *Woodstock*. Everyone started dreaming about a young woman emerging from behind the kerosene lamp. It felt like the days were going by slowly, while we sat around drinking icy water.

First thing one morning, Qu Er went out for a piss, but before he was done he came running back in screaming, "Woman!" A tentful of people abruptly sat up. At the foot of the slope was a young woman in a red headscarf, accompanied by an old guy on a donkey cart. What a gorgeous sight! The sun had just appeared high over the peaks, drenching her in its red glow, heating the snowy ground. She kept her head down shyly, the swiveling of her hips visible beneath the many layers of clothing that swaddled her, enough to shatter your heart. Her radiance was visible for miles, and she warmed us more than the sun.

The raw eggs stood at the tent entrance as though on the edge of a cliff, and if not for the white puffs of breath emerging from their mouths, you'd have thought they'd died on the spot. As the young woman drew closer, she glanced up at us. For me, a boy of eighteen or nineteen who hadn't seen a woman in more than thirty days, her eyes contained all things: big sister, mother, lover. I can still see those eyes now, the eyes of a true woman. They make me want to weep.

Anyway! Enough of that—I'm still not married, I haven't been able to find that pair of eyes again. They don't exist in the city. And I don't want to compromise—I'm a goddamn idealist. Perhaps it's all because of those eyes. That trip to the hills ruined me.

No! No more drinking. If I keep drinking, those eyes will be everywhere. Turn off the lights. Look, I'm crying. Please don't laugh at me.

CURE

In 1970, when I was with First Propaganda Unit in the Great Northern Waste, one of my comrades got a carbuncle on the back of his neck that refused to heal after several months. He had penicillin every day, but the rot persisted. The locals couldn't stand the sight, and finally one of them suggested a cure: chewing raw soybeans. Now this guy went around looking like he was making tofu with his jaws, white liquid swirling around his mouth. I asked how it tasted. Instead of answering, he handed me a soybean. It was pungent and acrid. This went on for seven days, and not only did he fail to get any better, he started farting in a variety of keys wherever he went. Turns out raw soybeans give you gas.

Another local told him a different trick: roast an old sow's dung till it's dry, mix it with "shaded soil" and egg white, apply to the affected area. The rest of us were certain the villagers had made this up as revenge against the educated youths for some misdeed or other and urged our friend not to listen. He was hesitant too, but the carbuncle bothered him so much, he decided he had to do whatever it took to treat it.

He got hold of a curved shard of tile, then followed a mother pig and her brood around. Whenever she had a bowel movement, he'd lunge forward and scoop it up. He only ever caught the end of it, but after four or five times, he had about enough. Next, he put a couple of bricks in the courtyard, balanced the tile on it, stuffed some dry grass underneath, and set it alight. Our dorm was over fifty meters away, and still we were awakened—that tells you how nasty the stench was. Taking one look at his panicked face, we bit back whatever words we'd been about to say. It really was the most godawful stink, almost supernatural.

Dried, the pigshit crumbled into powder. He then went round the rear of the building to scrape up some soil from the shaded ground there, cracked open a couple of eggs—precious commodities at the time—and separated them, stirring the whites into the mixture and ending up with something that actually did look like ointment.

It took some doing to get bandages from the medical center. The medic, who was from Tianjin, was thoroughly disgusted with what we were doing. She didn't understand why an educated youth would believe such superstitious rubbish. Abandoning perfectly good, clean medicines to trust in excrement, let alone *pig* excrement. This was no longer a question of hygiene, but fundamental values. This behavior was barbaric, primitive. At this point, she burst into tears. My carbuncled friend listened patiently, watched her cry, and finally said, The shit's been roasted, the germs are dead. Besides, I'm the one with the carbuncle, and I'm not crying, so you don't cry either, just give me the bandages. She stopped sobbing. Helpless in the face of his carbuncle, she handed over some bandages, insisting as she did so, I'm just providing the materials, if anything goes wrong I won't be responsible. My comrade thought about it for a moment and said, Fine.

A peculiar odor now filled our dorm, never allowing us to forget for one second what the ointment was made of. We didn't give him a hard time about that—sick people ought to be pitied. You could say every one of us was bearing the burden of this cure.

Fresh ointment had to be applied every other day. In less than a week, the pus had stopped flowing, the sore had closed up, and new flesh began growing in. His head, sunken for so long, could finally be held high again. When he played the flute, it no longer sounded like a sick person's moan. (He was a flautist in our orchestra.)

Some people said this had nothing to do with the "medicine," it was all the penicillin he'd already had. Others argued that a month of penicillin shots had done no good, while the shit had healed him right away. My friend didn't know either way, but he pursued the mother pig more energetically than before, enthusiastically making and applying more ointment. Sometime after that, I was transferred to the brigade propaganda team. There, I ran into an old buddy who now had armpit sores that just wouldn't heal. I told him about this cure, but he said he'd rather die. Later, he went back to Beijing and had surgery which cleared it up, though it also left him with a tendency to walk arms akimbo. Not everyone was able to accept this cure, and I didn't take it too seriously myself.

Then yesterday, I was flipping through a Tang dynasty compendium of herbal medicines, and in the fifteenth scroll of the animal section, I came across an item on the uses of pig dung: to cure fever, jaundice, and joint pain. And in smaller print: highly effective against rashes. So there it was. This hadn't come out of thin air, but was a prescription dating back to ancient times.

Everything in the world has a use. When I think about my friend running behind the pig with that shard of tile, I honestly have to respect him.

GRANULES

The place I was sent-down to was called Two Dragon Hill Village. North of Harbin, one stop before Dragon Town. The train only remained a couple of minutes at the station. A hurried stop.

I lived there for six years, every day different. I'll never again be able to lead such a life.

When I was a kid, I'd unwrap a candy, lick it once, wrap it up again, then unwrap it for another lick later. A single candy thus led to lingering pleasure. It was savored.

*

Tiemin never wore a hat. With his curly hair bare, he walked through the snow with his black violin case.

The case opened, and with a hum, he started teaching me to play. Open your Kayser, he said. Turn to page twenty-five, we'll start from bar eight.

*

Feng had asthma. Every morning he'd eat a mouthful of fresh ginger and a scoop of honey. Because he was ill, we all watched him eat. He was so slow it felt as if the honey wasn't sweet.

When he had nothing better to do, he'd get a sawblade and turn pieces of wood into washboards, carving patterns into them. One time, the board he'd just finished making got smashed when people nearby starting fighting. He found some paper, traced the pattern and did it all over again with a new piece of wood.

These washboards were made of basswood, an especially pale variety.

*

Big Eyes got his nickname from his large, protruding eyes, and whenever I saw him I would remember Mao's words, "The world is yours, as well as ours, but in the last analysis, it is yours." He cracked his knuckles non-stop as he spoke, *kak, kak, kak.* One finger at a time, left to right then right to left, all the way in one direction and then back.

One time, he told us *How the Steel Was Forged* was written by Ostrovsky. Such a long name, it sounded like it belonged to a noble, unfamiliar person.

*

Ni Wei could sing "Awaara Hoon" from the Bollywood film *Awaara.* He used to sing along with the record back in Beijing. He sang well, but not very often, and never taught us the lyrics. We loved that song, and once offered him a packet of Grape brand cigarettes if he'd teach it to us. He refused, claiming it was too hard to learn—but we knew it was so he could keep singing solo in the wheat fields, attracting the girls' attention.

We were so eager we made up our own nonsense version of the song. Annoyed, he went off and lay on a pile of stalks. We turned this melancholy ballad into a raucous romp. As we sang, the girls continued staring at him. He was chewing on some wheat grains.

*

Chen Gang had had meningitis, which left him a bit simple. One night, by the light of the kerosene lamps, he shouted, "I had a dream!" We asked him what about, and he said a fairy maiden. We asked what she'd been doing, and he said having a bath. That's when we realized Chen Gang might seem well-behaved, but he had a roguish side. We didn't ask any more questions, just tucked ourselves in well. We wanted to dream about fairy maidens too, though they didn't have to be bathing.

*

Yibin had run out of shoe polish, but he really wanted to go out on the town that night.

He tried rubbing his leather shoes with toothpaste. They didn't get any shinier, and now they smelled of spearmint.

Grabbing his shoes, he dashed out. I saw him rubbing them against a bullock's neck. The animal just stood there, apparently enjoying this.

His shoes gleamed and reeked strongly of cow.

*

In the twilight, Liu Wensheng boiled his underclothes in a basin, because all of us had fleas.

He'd recently fallen for Chu Ting from the pig-rearing team. He wanted to completely change his image, he said, to be mature and clean.

Distractedly, he boiled his clothes, stirring them with a twig. The dye ran, turning the murky water a dubious hue.

We eyed the contents of the basin and felt our bodies itch.

*

I was sitting beneath a poplar tree when Ma Ping returned from the southern hills. He gave me three little yellow fruits and said they were called Huang Taiping, "Huang" as in yellow. They were a little astringent, he said, a little sour.

I looked at the berries in the afternoon light but couldn't eat them. After a sniff, I tossed them away. Huang Taiping sounded too much like a person's name.

*

The district captain had a hand-cranked gramophone that took six No. 1 batteries. Every day, he listened to Linguaphone English records. Sometimes the belt slackened, coarsening the sound. The same thing happened if you played a 78 at 33 rpm: and if you did the opposite, it grew shrill. We kept wanting to play with his toy, until finally he started locking up the batteries. Even without them, the needle still moved across the record, producing a quiet sound. Tinier than our voices could ever produce.

*

We could never shit in peace—mosquitoes loved biting our bare bums. Once, Liu Wen ran back halfway through doing his business. Holding up a kerosene lamp, he asked Ma Ping to count the raised bumps on his ass. There were twenty-three. When Ma Ping was done counting, Liu Wen slumped against the heated kang platform, not moving, rather heavy hearted.

Ma Ping said, You ought to bring a couple of cigarettes with you when you shit, and keep blowing smoke behind you the whole time.

*

Mansheng went around in an army greatcoat, even though his father wasn't a big official or anything. We decided to beat him up one night. We got the Little Mute to lure him out, then went at him together, lobbing bricks and beer bottles at his head.

He collapsed before all of us had a chance to hit him.

None of us would have been able to take him on alone. He was bigger than all of us and had a party trick of filling a beer bottle with water and smacking the mouth to knock out the base.

The next day, his head was bandaged, but he still wore the greatcoat. The cafeteria made him a special meal for invalids: noodles with Sichuan peppercorn oil. Now he was even more eye-catching than before because of the bandages.

*

We poured water onto the courtyard to make a tiny ice rink, large enough for two or three. One night, I saw a girl skating wonderfully: Ren Xiaoyan from the Engineering Brigade.

I went back inside and wrote in my journal: . . . *You ought to have more determination. It's been three days, and you still haven't mastered skating backward. Even the oldies who started later are about to overtake you. From tomorrow, you have to practice three hours a day, never mind how cold it is or how tired you are. . . . If there's not enough time during the day, carry on training at night.*

I ran back outside after writing that entry, but Ren Xiaoyan was gone.

*

Miao Quan hopped a goods train to Beijing. It didn't stop at our station, but he jumped on board and departed with a wave of his empty satchel.

The sky darkened as the train sped away. I walked alone through the snow. It took me what felt like half the night to get back to the dorm.

As I burrowed beneath the covers, I could smell my own stench beneath the blanket.

*

It was dawn when we came back from unloading cement. Ma Ping said, Let's not sleep, we'll go buy hats in Dedu county town. So we headed there. He got a shearling hat, I got a dogskin one.

On the way back, I pillowed my head on the dogskin and went to sleep. When I woke up, I found a trail of drool on my new hat. Ma Ping had stayed awake—he hadn't wanted to let down the flaps of his hat, so he'd sat motionless with it perched on top of his head. It was indeed a very expensive hat.

*

Wu Zhaoyi had had polio and walked with a limp. Everyone called him Do-Re-Mi. He was good at chess, and he sniffled as he played so snot wouldn't dribble onto his shirt. When he went to the province for a tournament, Dr. Li gave him a couple of antihistamines. He took them, and though his nose did stop running, he then slumped over the chessboard and fell asleep.

*

Wen Jie played Little Changbao in *Taking Tiger Mountain*, but she could never hit the high notes, so Ma Li sang them backstage. Not content to go unrecognized, she started stepping forward beyond the curtains so everyone could see she was doing it. Wen Jie got upset and her performance suffered. In the end, Ma Li took over the part of Little Changbao, but the audience found it weird seeing her in the role.

*

Wang Guangfu, an educated youth from Tianjin, wrote my classmate Feng Li a note: *If you're willing, when we meet at the cafeteria tomorrow, I'll say, "What nice weather today," and you'll say, "I'm an educated youth from Beijing." If you'd rather not, please don't respond.*

The next day, Wang Guangfu got his food, then hung around waiting for Feng Li to get hers too. Looking out the window, he said in a trembling voice, "What nice weather today." Eight of the girls from Feng Li's dorm replied in unison, "I'm an educated youth from Beijing."

Wang Guangfu didn't finish his meal. He knew Feng Li had told everyone about his note.

Later, he went to Bei'an and tried to kill himself, stabbing himself two or three times with a knife, though he didn't die. Everyone thought he'd done it because of the prank those girls played on him. The girls didn't agree, but when Wang Guangfu returned, they all just so happened to be away on family visits.

*

Granules are different from pearls, which have holes in them and can be strung up. If you scatter granules across the floor, you have to pick them up one by one. True memories are more granule than pearl—there's no string that links them neatly together. Granules can ferment into stories, but stories are steamed buns, white and pillowy, not granular at all. Yunju Temple in Beijing's Fangshan district has Buddhist relics that are said to emit light once every few centuries. They're a sort of granule too, the crystallization of what remains after burning. I've studied them up close, but they still seemed unimaginably far away, beyond the reach of my life and imagination. Buddhist relics are left behind as a sort of essence, the result of life-long contemplation. It took countless days and nights of food, drink, thought, scripture, shit, and so forth to produce them. These tiny things, like grains of sand, will never disappear. There's no tragedy, no romance, no politics here. They're there when you see them, gone when you don't.

MALINGERING

1.

The sensation of walking into a hospital is always the same. Do it ten years later and there'd be no difference. Maybe because the medicinal odor is identical, and the eyes of sick people, and the doctors striding around as if they were the Savior himself. The only difference is sometimes you're a healthy person obliged to visit the hospital for one reason or another, and sometimes you really are ill. As a genuine patient, you notice that doctors are like antique experts, probing your mouth, evaluating the color of your tongue, the icy imprint of their stethoscopes on your chest and back, the instrument warm by the time they remove it. Only after all this do they ask what's wrong. Then they say the name of the illness you already had in your mind, scribble out a prescription, and send you to the cashier for processing. You pay your fee, get your medicine, swallow your pills. This is the procedure for a straightforward visit to the doctor.

My biggest operation to date has been a tooth extraction—a particularly inglorious episode while I was in the Great Northern Waste. I'd been so exhausted I was ready to faint. In order to get a couple of days' rest, I decided to sacrifice one of my good innermost teeth. The dentist was an educated youth who'd only had a few days of training. When I said I wanted a tooth removed, she tried to hide her nervousness by fiddling non-stop with the hammer and chisel in her hands, attempting to resemble an experienced stonemason. This caused me to question, amid my panic, whether this proedure would be worth it. As she anesthetized me, she named acupressure points I'd never heard of, claiming that injecting the top gum would produce better results. After twenty minutes, she began work, tapping and prizing away. I screamed in such pain she was forced to stop. Going over the dosage and process of injecting me, she reckoned it shouldn't have hurt. I really was in agony, though. She said there was nothing for it but to use acupuncture. This was a fashionable method at the time—you can see it in movies of the period. She jabbed silver needles around my mouth, and the tiny prickles of pain calmed me down. The subsequent extraction was like tearing down a wall or pouring concrete. My job was to hold my head still, not moving even as the hammer came down. This was difficult. The educated youth was sweating now, and I seriously regretted trying to obtain a couple of days' rest through a method even more painful than the forced labor I was avoiding. Finally, the tooth got banged out, but its root stayed behind. I looked at the bloody fragments and stopped her before she could even think of digging out the remnants.

Breathing hard, she wrote out a three-day medical excuse for me. I spent those three days eating boiled noodles—the sort with Sichuan peppercorn oil sprinkled on them. I worried that I'd be stuck eating soft noodles for the rest of my life. More than ten years later, the tooth stump still throbs every now and then, a penetrating, vigorous pain that makes me think of work tools.

2.

If the Railroad Hospital still holds my medical records, you'll be able to read about my most serious illness there: a prolapsed lumbar disc. This was the reason I was able to leave the Henan farming village in Ruyang county, where I'd been since 1975, after being redeployed from the Great Northern Waste. I then returned to Beijing, no longer an educated youth but a worker with an urban hukou. In reality, though, I never had this ailment.

Most people don't know the term "medical discharge," referring to educated youths being returned to the cities from the farming villages they were sent to due to health reasons.

During that time, I searched constantly for something to be wrong with me, something difficult to detect yet serious enough to get me sent home. Most of my medical knowledge was gained during this period, from a book called *The Barefoot Doctor's Guide*. This publication was very widely read, perhaps as much as the yellow almanacs in the old days. It contained a number of shocking photographs—syphilis, chancre sores, and so on—teaching me a great deal about venereal disease as well. The government was claiming STDs had been eliminated from the country, and we hadn't heard of HIV yet, so it's unclear what purpose these pictures served. When I selected a prolapsed lumbar disc as my fake illness, I took care to memorize all the literature. I knew back to front what tests would be carried out and the symptoms I should exhibit. When I presented myself at the Railroad Hospital, I could tell from the way he examined me that my surgeon was very experienced. There were no pictures of this condition in my book because it consisted entirely of symptoms: being unable to lift your lower leg while lying flat, being unable to bend your big toe inward, frequent shooting pains through your legs, soreness while passing motion or coughing. After my examination, I was pronounced a most suitable patient—and even afterward, as I came down from the examining table, I spent a further five minutes continuing to creakily play this part, convinced in that moment I really was unwell. The doctor wrote out his diagnosis—this wasn't easy to obtain, and must have been at least half-motivated by compassion. He knew I was an educated youth.

In 1977, having finally acquired the status of a sick person, I returned in good health, eight years after I was first sent away from the city. Medical discharges would become the main reason educated youths were able to return home. Many of them had strange, obscure ailments, able to fool even lab tests or X-rays.

It's different now. These days, I've reached the age when illnesses find me without any need for pretense. I seldom go to the hospital, not even for a check-up, because every word the doctors say makes me shiver with fright.

SUCH A WOMAN, SUCH CLOTH

In 1977, I was deployed to a hill village in Henan. The women in this place, before they got married, would weave huge quantities of coarse fabric—for bedcovers, for padded jackets, for undershirts. Before this, they had to pull clumps of cotton wool into shreds, then sit at a wooden loom and send the shuttle back and forth, foot on the treadle up and down, all to produce something the thickness of a single thread.

This took place at night. During the day, everyone was busy on the land. If they had nothing else to do in the evenings, they would sit in the courtyard weaving away. They never lit a lamp. If the moon was shining, they would work by moonlight; if not, they would feel their way in the dark, treadles thudding away late into the night.

One spring, just as the locust flowers were blossoming, I crossed the unlit street. Floral fragrance all around me, the sound of weaving in my ear. The loom sounded remote and isolated by night, punctuated now and then by footsteps. The quieter it was, the more it seemed to belong to a different era. I don't know who the weaver was that night, and I never found out, but I've always imagined she must have been the most beautiful woman, like the one in the poem "Reeds."

After the cloth was woven, it still needed to be colored. If dye was unaffordable, they would gather ore and boil it with the fabric.

The resultant hue would not be vibrant, but the same dull red-brown as the earth. The fabric would then be brought to the river and left there, a long stretch of water with a long strip of cloth floating in it, so many days flowing away. There was a girl who went down to the river with her cloth, who never seemed to smile. She walked down the street carrying the bale, melancholy beauty in her posture.

Soon, she would be gone from this street. After the autumn harvest, she would cross the pavement one last time, and go over to the hills with a man. Keeping the fires burning, planting seeds, getting through winter, getting through summer . . . and hand-woven cloth would accompany her constantly, garments by day, covers by night.

Why that man? No matter how many times he came over, he still seemed as distant as a star. Would the coarse fabric be laid over his body too, layer after layer of warp and weft swaddling him, all those hand-dyed colors?

Night after night, weaving away, but the man cannot be woven into existence. He's hidden in the fabric, and when you're sad you clutch him and weep.

On the ice-cold water, the cloth drifts a long way. These stretches of river hold a dull red tinge, a red that can never be gathered up again. These colors have slipped from the cloth and dispersed far away. You'll never get them back.

After the cloth has been dipped in the river, it needs to be hung on a bamboo rack to dry. When that's done, it will have shrunk quite a bit, and the color will be paler. Holding it in your hand, it feels like time made visible. So many threads you couldn't pluck loose if you wanted, they're part of the cloth now. Sniff. You smell water, moonlight, sunlight—and time.

Nothing has ever been this clear. Such a woman, such cloth.

AUNTIE XIN

Auntie Xin never gave the dog a name. Other people called their dogs Blackie or Chrysanthemum, but hers was just "Dog." When she went out and it tried to follow she'd holler, Dog, go back! It'd stand there for a while, until she called again, Dog, go back! And then it would go. She called her chickens "Chicken," shouting "Chicken Chicken Chicken" at feeding time so they'd come running. Auntie Xin also had a cat, which she named "Spot."

Once, Spot attacked a chicken. Auntie Xin saw this and snatched the bird from her. It was headless by then. Auntie Xin stared at the decapitated creature and muttered, This stuff, this stuff. She boiled some water and plucked the bird, cleaning out its guts, and fried it up. When she'd filled a plate with meat, she came to call me, Come and eat this stuff.

I didn't quite dare eat the chicken, not because of Auntie Xin's "this stuff," but the uncertain circumstances of its death. I may have been hungry, but things weren't so bad I would have eaten a sick chicken. After finding different ways of politely declining, I grew frantic. Still she insisted, It's just a chicken the cat killed, eat it, it's not like it was your pet.

So I ate, managing to forget sickness and death, chewing with vigor.

People in Ruyang used to kill dogs by stuffing calcium carbide into a sweet potato, which a hungry dog would gobble down. The calcium carbide exploded on contact with moisture—you could tell by the steam this emitted. Dogs who'd eaten calcium carbide suffered a lot, dying slowly. Some lingered in agony for a whole day.

Someone did this to Auntie Xin's dog. It was fine when it went out in the morning, but a while later it came stumbling back. Auntie Xin was feeding the pigs but dropped the pail when she saw the dog's wounded eyes. Dog! she screamed. It held itself upright, not moving at all. She fetched it a piece of black bread, and the dog raised its head to look at her.

She rushed out into the courtyard and began screaming energetically, A decent person wouldn't hurt a dumb animal. You bastard, I hope you get reincarnated as a dog and blown up! Not many people were passing by, so it looked like she was screaming at the local farmers.

The dog, holding itself gingerly, stumbled out of the courtyard, as if displaying its torment to help Auntie Xin. She looked at it and started shouting again, tears streaming, Dog, you're so useless, why would you take food from a blackhearted villain? Dog, I'm so sorry, it's all my fault for not feeding you enough. You're a good dog, please don't die, a good dog wouldn't die, don't give those bastards the satisfaction!

At noon, more people showed up and Auntie Xin's scolding grew sorrowful. No one tried to calm her down. Everyone watched the shivering dog, debating whether it might survive.

The dog suddenly lurched toward the stream that flowed past the front door, standing in the shallow water with its fur wet, its silence increasing the volume and sadness of Auntie Xin's tirade. Some of the watchers went down to the river to lift the dog out, but as soon as they'd done this it charged back in, as if determined to increase the tragedy of the moment.

Someone started to curse whoever had harmed this dog. The dog stood in the stream, motionless. It probably recognized the person who'd hurt it but didn't point them out. More people arrived to stare at the dog, waiting for it to pass out. When that happened, Auntie Xin's words would grow less powerful, lacking the dog's silence to give them force.

Ignored by the crowd, Auntie Xin stopped crying. She didn't know what to do next. She wished the dog would collapse at a suitable time, giving her another opportunity to lash out.

But that didn't happen. It got to evening, time to stop work, and the dog still stood in the stream. Everyone who walked past muttered, Why's that dog not dead yet? To think it's still alive!

After dinner, Auntie Xin came out to see how the dog was doing. She said, Dog, what's going on? . . . Dog. Then she walked back inside and shut the courtyard door.

It died during the night, no one knew when. The next day, we saw its bulky carcass floating in the stream. Silent, head submerged.

BECAUSE OF MENDELSSOHN

One day at the subway station, you hear Mendelssohn's *Concerto in E Minor*, and instinctively touch the four fingertips of your left hand—they're smooth, the calluses gone without a trace. No one would be able to tell you'd once played the violin, practicing eight hours a day, beginning with a slow gliding across open strings, using your whole bow, over and over, the instrument squawking like an undead chicken from G to E and back again. Day after day, knowing all the while how far from you the music was . . .

The Mendelssohn continues. You can't hide from its grace and purity any more than you can escape failure . . .

Next, you learned scales, positions, staccato, spiccato, harmonics, vibrato. From Kreutzer to Jakob Dont, tadpole-like music notes swallowed many years, during which the vast illusion of musicianship enfolded you. You read the stories of Paganini, of Jascha Heifetz, of David Fyodorovich Oistrakh. You felt that someday, possibly, perhaps, maybe, who knows . . .

You brought your violin along to the Great Northern Waste. These vast plains required a sturdy pair of hands, you couldn't possibly speak to poverty-stricken farmers about hands or Paganini. You tilled the land in the summer, harvested the wheat in the autumn, spread frozen manure in the winter. When your fingers pressed the strings, the sounds they produced weren't as solid as before. They no longer obeyed you. Bit by bit, your violin began to feel like a congealed dream.

Mendelssohn's *Concerto in E Minor* also feels like a dream . . .

During this time, art was an extravagance. On the threshing floor, going through repetitive motions, you remembered the melody of *Introduction* and *Rondo Capriccioso* and hummed it quietly. Following the beat, you raised your metal flail and brought it down on the plump grains, up then down again. In an instant, it hit you fully how far you all were from the life of the imagination.

The Mendelssohn plays on, and this time round you don't need to worry about it being interrupted by a snippet from a Revolutionary tune . . .

One evening, you were summoned from your dorm, and a stern-faced official said to you, Fetch your instrument and report to headquarters, you're needed to rehearse a model opera—a glorious, arduous Revolutionary duty. You'll start tomorrow.

You went back to your dorm and retrieved your violin, wiping off the dust. The strings were loose, and when you tightened them, a hum rose from deep within its body, as if it was yawning after being roused. When you were done tuning, you set it down and examined your hands. The calluses were there, but no longer on your fingertips—they were now on your palms.

In *Taking Tiger Mountain*, a long overture precedes the final assault, with sixteenth notes coming thick and fast. Such a vigorous piece of music certainly couldn't be performed by just one violin—that would be far too thin a sound. All the instruments take part, so you hear the scattered troops galloping through the air around you. Apart from the haplessness of everyone trying their utmost, you heard no music. You said this wouldn't do, all the instruments should go back to practicing scales. No one paid any attention. An orchestra with only eleven days to rehearse an entire opera had no reason to heed talk of going back to basics. And the show came together, a heartfelt miracle.

The Mendelssohn changes, growing more magnificent, shimmering. . . .

It's not like you could just play Mendelssohn any time you wanted. That day, resting after the performance, you sat beneath a catalpa tree, running through some exercises. Your fingers had recovered their former strength, and you began a Mendelssohn piece, sinking into it with something like hopefulness. The propaganda bureau chief, there for an inspection, happened to hear you. He asked, What kind of song are you playing on that fiddle? (He insisted on calling your instrument a "fiddle.") You told him. He said, Who's this Mendelssohn, then? You explained. He said, Ah, no wonder it sounds like some stinking bourgeois barroom tune; if you've got nothing better to do, why not play *Taking Tiger Mountain*? Or a piece that tells a Revolutionary story, like *The Flowing River*? Or better yet, learn the erhu, you'll be much closer to the People that way.

The righteousness of his bringing up the erhu and the People left you speechless. You put away your violin; you looked at it lying flat in its case, a corpse ready for burial.

From that day, I began keeping a diary. In a corner of my upper bunk each day, I wrote all that was within me. No matter how late it was, even if it was just one line, I wrote. I grew mesmerized by these white pages that kept my feelings safe, words even more comforting than music notes, although they were silent, and only I could hear them. When I'd almost filled my first notebook, an educated youth from Shanghai sneaked a look. He left a note behind, stuck between the pages: *Your journal moved me deeply—you said many things that I've wanted to, and I hope you keep writing, but nothing too revealing. A Revolutionary salute—you know who.*

Thinking about it, that would make him my first reader, the first person to encourage me. I knew what he meant about being too revealing. After that, my entries often took the form of poetry, only recording emotional states. I once wrote the words, "Wind, bitterly cold white hair." Looking at it now, this line seems horribly affected.

I started with a sort of complete self-awareness, which was different from the violin. There was no music score to follow, and I never dreamed I'd be able to bring my writing and my life together. It was more like a discussion, a dialogue with a blank sheet of paper, squeezing a few words from my heart each time. The flow of words when talking to myself was touching for someone who wanted to say something but couldn't get the words out.

I kept writing until I left the Great Northern Waste.

Now I see this was just a beginning, one that had to do with abandoning the violin, although to this day I haven't been able to claim that was what set me on my present path. That wouldn't be an honest account.

I returned to Beijing in 1977, aged twenty-five. There were all kinds of possibilities ahead of me, and in fact I tried many of them. For three years, I worked hard to attain a life of mundane stability. After that, I went back to writing, throwing my whole self into it. Those who knew me well were surprised by my dedication. In an essay about writing, I once said: Anyone who still wants to write poetry after the age of thirty must be doing it for an inescapable reason. What my reason is, I have no idea, but it's something to do with my life, my very existence. I'm happy to accept this way of describing it: people who write are destined to write, and no matter what they've been through in their lives, they'll still end up writing in the end.

More than a decade had passed, and poetry entered my life. I've only ever been grateful that it chose to do so.

I walk out of the subway station, and Mendelssohn disappears. Now I think about art and how it never paused, nor could ever be interrupted. Once again, I have no calluses on my left hand. Instead, there are fleshy pads on my right, where I grip my pen.

AFTERWORD

The hourglass has been turned over, and yesterday's sand comes rushing back, the same sand, every last grain. One's passing days are like an hourglass, and not "like a flowing river," as the sage says, slipping by never to return. Time repeats itself. Today and yesterday, this year and last year, not one grain of sand that goes by is unfamiliar to you. Such days bring a word to mind: mundane. Most people inevitably lead mundane lives, whether reluctantly or willingly. (After all, he who stood at the prow of a boat lamenting the flowing water was a great poet.)

You hear "youth is a little bird that flies away never to return" and apply the words to yourself, realizing your youth departed along with your broken tooth. At fortunate moments, you fix your eyes on the nest and watch birds taking off in silhouette. These shadows aren't grains of sand, nor are they flowing water, they are shadows. The past and the future are equally unreachable.

In the hourglass, you do your best to experience disappearance. The emptied-out space is heavier, awaiting replenishment, while some memories cannot be lightened. The void is above the truth, utterly clear.

After this account, it's gone. You've handed over your past, and no longer have any way to fill the void. Nothing to flip through. When you look in the mirror, you see a transparent person moving in and out of life. Your life grows even more mundane, and you tire of the topsy-turvy hourglass.

Everyone has a vast book in their heart, its beginning very far away. The wise do not read it out. You, mundane and hollow, spend your savings. You see light seeping from the tangible sand, and the empty space grows larger and larger.

POEMS

White Horse

A white horse trots on the high slope
His white body absorbs the dark night
He leads the entire snowy plain
Into the crisp morning
White horse, white life
Melting into the snowy plain
Heading into deeper winter
Body like snow piled high by wind
A white horse in the distance
On the snowy plain
Coat greenish in the spring
With clusters of wildflowers
In the screaming wind the white horse
Vanishes
The wooden cart
Empty with a white horse's waiting

Spring Grass

Spring grass on last year's old ground
Green, in the dawn of the staging post
Recalling the moment of being forgotten
New spring grass is green
Frail, steadfast. She's green
Those who see her lower their heads
On a piece of earth sensitive to the sun
Spring grass, new green infants
Leaving those used to winter
At a loss, their fires put out
Watching spring grass reach up high
More desolate than the snowy ground
Each year spring grass is heard by the northern bells
Seen by the seeds far within
Each year's spring grass is different
For instance, this year it's heavy with sadness

Darhan's Moon

You draw me closer to the celestial court
Darhan your distant name
Draws me closer to the moon
On such a night, vast, solitary
Darhan you ignore fires and human voices
Dark and still as always
Darhan's moon, overhead light
Is it shining on me? Or else the plains
Shift the light from my body
Darhan's moon, you make ten thousand years
Feel like this night
Same wind, same grass
Same magnificent desolation
Same Darhan
Who is strong enough to enter you, call you
And make you reply

n.b. Darhan is a semi-arid region of Inner Mongolia

Squall

A night when crow-dark clouds gather
Snowy fields lonely and cold
A horse chews night grass
Pricks up its ears
Hears the wind rattle
Farmers' doors and windows

Starfish

Died just like that
On the beach
Still glistening
Dried and stonelike
In this way
It refuses to pretend
But shoots its rage
In five directions

Spirit or What Some People Argue

Fling a bird into feathers
And its body rises so very high
A bird on paper strikes the same pose
But the background isn't blue enough
It makes me think in silence of true flight
A sort of swift vanishing
Say it again and you could put it like this:
If you haven't vanished from humanity, you've never soared

Summoning an Ox

The wind blows across
The weary silence of the fields
Searching for a missing ox
Armed with provisions   Walking a long way
The sky like any other day
Sometimes clouded
Sometimes clear and borderless
This season has no birds, no rain
The scent of the earth slowly fades
The season when snow and frost will soon arrive
Summoning that ox
Like an autumn evening
A mother shouting into the wilderness, calling her children home

Train

Night, snow drifting
So airy, so pure
Near the tracks
Lights on the hillside
A passenger train approaches
This I know
For days I've awaited it at this hour
Standing here like this
Snow on the ground steadfastly cold
A gleaming passenger train
Heading south, each window flashing past
Cozy, unfamiliar
I see people standing, walking around
Their destination is past the city of my birth
But I cannot go with them
The train passes by
Swift, chaotic
I no longer hear metal on metal
Standing there
Snow underfoot spreading farther
Spreading snow even quieter

Nightsong

The night is a stranger
I'm usually in dreamland then
But tonight I can't sleep
Outside the stars are cold enough to crack
Clinging to a thread of light
I quietly shrug on slumbering clothes
The clock strikes
Silence descends again
Grope my way out of the room
Outside is fresh breeze and freedom
I stare a long time at the north
Where the night still glimmers
Maybe it's an illusion
I often think of silver birches and snow
On such a night, facing a skyful of galaxies
Who feels the same way I do?

Dirge

I will die on an autumn evening
The hour when silence arrives
Soil awaits ripe fruit
The strength of autumn, whose hands can receive all of this
After death I will enter the dawn
A different radiance, sunrise
Humanity awakening, no longer the same
My warmth will embrace the sun's
I will hear my final wind and cock crow
Departing the earth
In autumn what can deter
Ripeness and determination

ZOU JINGZHI is highly regarded in China as a fiction writer, poet, essayist, screenwriter, and playwright. He is a founding member of the Chinese theater collective Longmashe. As a screenwriter, the films he wrote for Zhang Yimou and Wong Kar Wai have been well received at film festivals across the world. His plays and operas have been performed in China as well as internationally, and his poems and essays have been very influential, going into multiple reprints.

JEREMY TIANG has translated over twenty books from Chinese, including novels by Yan Ge, Yeng Pway Ngon, Zhang Yueran, Shuang Xuetao, Lo Yi-Chin, Chan Ho-Kei, and Geling Yan. His novel *State of Emergency* won the Singapore Literature Prize in 2018. He also writes and translates plays. Originally from Singapore, he now lives in New York City.

CPSIA information can be obtained
at www.ICGtesting.com
Printed in the USA
JSHW082310110723
44616JS00004B/12